BOOK TWO
JUNIPER SPARK
AND THE UNRAVELING

To: Piper Jo ♡
Share your LIGHT!
♡ Courtney

BOOK TWO

JUNIPER SPARK
— AND —
THE UNRAVELING

COURTNEY WOODRUFF

COVER & MAP DESIGN BY MEFORYA (MEHNAAZ H.)

Foster Hollow
PRESS

Text and Artwork Copyright © 2023 Courtney Woodruff
Cover and Map Design by Meforya (Mehnaaz H.)

Paperback ISBN-13: 978-1-7368290-7-3
Also available in eBook

Copyright notice: All rights reserved under the International and Pan-American Copyright Conventions. No part of this book may be reproduced or transmitted in any form or by any means, electronic or mechanical, including photocopying and recording, or by any information storage and retrieval system, without permission in writing from the publisher.

This is a work of fiction. Names, places, characters, and incidents are either the product of the author's imagination or are used fictitiously, and any resemblance to any actual persons, living or dead, organizations, events, or locales is entirely coincidental.

Warning: the unauthorized reproduction or distribution of this copyrighted work is illegal. Criminal copyright infringement, including infringement without monetary gain, is investigated by the FBI and is punishable by up to 5 years in prison and a fine of $250,000.

*To my parents, grandparents,
aunts, and uncles.
Thank you for your stories,
your legacies of faith,
and for giving me glimpses of
what God's love looks like on earth.*

CAST OF CHARACTERS

SPARK FAMILY

- **Alder Spark (Lord):** Red squirrel; Juniper and Jasper's grandfather; loyal to King Cypress
- **Aspen Spark (Deceased):** Red squirrel; Juniper and Jasper's great-grandfather; member of the First Alliance
- **Hawthorn Spark (Lieutenant Colonel):** Red squirrel; Juniper and Jasper's father; went missing in action during the Unraveling, and has not been seen in fourteen years
- **Hemlock Spark (General):** Red squirrel; Juniper and Jasper's uncle; highest-ranking Archer
- **Hickory Spark (Chief Guardian):** Red squirrel; highest-ranking Dark Forest Guardian; Juniper and Jasper's uncle
- **Jasper Spark (Captain):** Red squirrel; Juniper's brother; grew up at Logan Bramble under Hemlock's care; attended Bramble Academy; climber and Archer
- **Juniper Spark:** Red squirrel; left in Sorrel's care at Foster Hollow as an infant; rumored to be the prophesied squirrel that will save Mirren from King Cypress and Lords of Prey
- **Laurel (Warbler) Spark**: Red squirrel; Juniper and Jasper's mother; believed to have been in hiding since the Unraveling

FOSTER HOLLOW RESIDENTS

- **Birch:** Douglas squirrel; Juniper's foster brother
- **Douglas "Dougie":** Douglas squirrel; Juniper's foster brother
- **Fern:** Red squirrel; Juniper's foster brother
- **Poppy:** Douglas squirrel; Juniper's foster sister
- **Rose "Rosie":** Ground squirrel; Juniper's infant foster sister
- **Sorrel:** Gray squirrel; Foster Hollow caretaker; Juniper's foster mom; correspondent for the cause

ORDER OF THE ARCHERS

Logan Bramble (Archer Headquarters)

- **Rhododendron "Rhodie" (Corporal):** Field mouse; burrower; member of Captain Jasper Spark's team
- **Sitka (Sergeant):** Red fox; ranger; member of Captain Jasper Spark's team
- **Willow (Private):** Anna's Hummingbird; flier; member of Captain Jasper Spark's team

Camp Marshall (Archer Training Grounds)

- **Ash (Cadet):** Gray squirrel; Juniper's foster brother; climber trainee; former Dark Forest Guardian trainee; under probation for sharing Foster Hollow's secret location with Lords of Prey

Camp Marshall (Archer Training Grounds), cont'd...

- **Clover (Sergeant):** Hare; leader of Camp Marshall burrower unit
- **Dahlia (Cadet):** Fruit bat; Juniper's bunk mate at Camp Marshall; flier trainee; member of last known bat family living in the Dark Forest
- **Dandelion (Cadet):** Mole; burrower trainee
- **Daphne (Cadet):** Bobcat; ranger trainee; orphan of the Unraveling; attended Bramble Academy
- **Holly (Cadet):** Wren; flier trainee
- **Huckleberry (Cadet):** Pine marten; ranger trainee
- **Lavender (Cadet):** Gopher; burrower trainee
- **Maple (Cadet):** Red-headed woodpecker; flier trainee
- **Moss (Sergeant):** Swallow; leader of the Camp Marshall flier unit
- **Oak (Cadet):** Pine marten; ranger trainee
- **Pine (Sergeant):** Raccoon; leader of Camp Marshall ranger unit
- **Pollen (Sergeant):** Fox squirrel; leader of Camp Marshall climber unit at Camp Marshall
- **Seed (Cadet):** Hedgehog; burrower trainee; orphan of the Unraveling; raised at Logan Bramble
- **Spikerush "Spike" (Cadet):** Gray squirrel; climber trainee; orphaned by the Lords of Prey
- **Thistle (Colonel):** Cardinal; highest-ranking Camp Marshall officer

LORDS OF PREY

- **Agate (Lord):** Badger; ally of Lord Alder; loyal to King Cypress
- **Cypress (King):** Wolf; self-proclaimed King of Mirren
- **Fleabane (Commander):** Coyote; highest-ranking member of the King's Guard (shares role with his brother, Skullcap)
- **Larkspur:** Red-tailed hawk; Lords of Prey page and messenger; loyal to King Cypress
- **Sedge (Lord):** Red fox; Sitka and Spruce's father; loyal to King Cypress
- **Skullcap (Commander):** Coyote; highest-ranking member of the King's Guard (shares role with his brother, Fleabane)
- **Spruce:** Red fox; Sitka's brother; Sedge's son; loyal to King Cypress

FIRST ALLIANCE

- **Flint the Black:** Grizzly bear; last-known living member of the First Alliance; sworn protector of the Spark family; Aspen's best friend

OLD MIRREN

- **Oleander:** Screech owl; prophet who predicted a red squirrel would save Mirren from King Cypress and Lords of Prey

CONTENTS

PROLOGUE / 15
ONE: SHAMBLES / 17
TWO: FLASH OF RED / 27
THREE: BITTER BLACKBERRIES / 33
FOUR: THE WARBLERS / 43
FIVE: SMOKE / 53
SIX: HEMLOCK'S REQUEST / 59
SEVEN: ABOUT FACE / 63
EIGHT: CAMP MARSHALL / 73
NINE: CAPTAIN SPARK / 87
TEN: ARCHER VALUES / 97
ELEVEN: MERCY / 105
TWELVE: FAILURE & FORGIVENESS / 115
THIRTEEN: GRADUATION DAY / 129
FOURTEEN: RICHIE GORGE / 137
FIFTEEN: FOUND & LOST / 147
SIXTEEN: SITKA'S SECRET / 157
SEVENTEEN: JASPER'S JEALOUSY / 165
EIGHTEEN: JUNIPER'S UNRAVELING / 171
EPILOGUE / 175
SNEAK PEEK / 181
ACKNOWLEDGEMENTS / 184

PROLOGUE

"The ranks are ready, my king," Lord Alder bows low, addressing the great wolf and his pair of coyote companions. Despite the elder squirrel's hardened expression, the sour stench of anxiety gives away his true disposition with each nervous twitch of his bushy, red-orange tail.

Cypress nods, trying not to salivate at the enticing scent. He looks down from his rocky perch, admiring the vast army assembled in the canyon beneath him. He can hear the snarls of restless creatures, all claws and teeth, echoing off granite walls over the roar of rushing water. "Took you long enough. There will be severe consequences if you miss the mark this time."

"Yes, King Cypress." Alder bows once more, his wooden armor scraping the silvery rock beneath his feet. Without another word, he turns to retreat down the cliffside. Cypress, along with the two highest ranking members of his King's Guard, Commanders Fleabane and Skullcap, watch Lord Alder with interest until he disappears over the treacherous precipice.

"I've got a craving for squirrel," the coyote seated to the king's left growls.

"Quit drooling, Fleabane," the wolf warns. "He's Aspen's son."

"He'll taste that much more savory," Commander Fleabane licks his teeth. A bone shard flies at him from the right, barely nicking his snout. He lets out a yip of pain.

"Alder is the only one left who knows the secrets of the Tree," Commander Skullcap, the coyote seated on the other side of Cypress, reminds his partner.

"Right," Fleabane whines, rubbing his stinging nose with the back of his paw. "I forgot."

"Have patience," Cypress says. "We will each have what is ours in due time."

ONE
SHAMBLES

Juniper is not prepared for what's waiting for her at Foster Hollow. She once believed the series of complicated locks made her home impenetrable to trespassers. The rattling clank of each latch clicking into place had helped her sleep soundly as a young kit and feel safe from whatever beasts lurk in the Dark Forest after curfew. Now, the heavy, wooden door dangles from the tree like a loose tooth.

Juniper's heart leaps when Uncle Hickory's husky form reemerges from the shadowy doorway of the abandoned woodpecker nest that had been transformed into a foster home for young squirrels. Having insisted upon being the first ones to enter, he and her brother, Jasper, had swept the Hollow for hidden dangers before they would allow Juniper to come inside.

"It's clear," Hickory says. "But you're not going to like what you see."

Foster Hollow is in shambles, she remembers her brave friend, Rhodie, the armor-clad field mouse, sharing her report of the damage that had been done to Juniper's home in a weasel attack. At that moment, Juniper had pictured upside-down furniture and scattered knick knacks. Now, the soft red hairs on the back of her neck stand up with dread. She wonders what she will find beyond the empty doorframe.

The young squirrel holds her breath and steps over the threshold, barely hearing her uncle call down to Flint the Black to let him know it's safe. The great bear had asked—demanded, rather—to accompany the small crew on their dangerous trek from Logan Bramble. Riding upon the grizzly's broad shoulders, the trip through the Dark Forest hadn't taken nearly as long as Juniper remembered.

"All is clear down here," Flint calls up to the squirrels from the shade of a fallen tree where he'd already begun dozing. "Take your time."

Comforted by the grizzly bear standing guard, snoring or not, Juniper takes another step inside. Her eyes slowly adjust to the dimness of the great circular room that makes up the kitchen, dining room, and living area.

She has never seen this space without the warm glow of a candle or dancing fireplace embers. The absence of her foster mother, Sorrel, is felt in the jarring chill and silence radiating from the walls. There is a damp, earthy stench in the air. She recognizes the stink of spoiled food and mildew, but there's something else. Something putrid.

"What's that smell?" Juniper shudders, wrinkling her nose.

Jasper makes a gagging sound and lifts his foot to shake off whatever he's just stepped in. "Weasel droppings," he chokes in disgust. Juniper's stomach turns.

The living room comes into focus. Sofa cushions are turned inside out, fluff spilling onto the scratched wooden floor. Fireplace ashes have been sifted through, and piles of soot darken the cozy rug where little Dougie's blocks lie scattered. She bends down to retrieve a few of them, tucking them into the knapsack she had slung over one shoulder. Dougie will be happy to be reunited with his favorite toys.

She crosses the dining room to the kitchen, trying not to let her eyes linger on the long table where her foster family has shared so many happy meals. Ugly claw marks mar the polished surface. Her stomach flips when she notices every cabinet door is hanging from its hinges, and drawers lie splintered on the kitchen floor. Soiled pots and pans Sorell had used to prepare Juniper's birthday meal are still in the sink, fuzzy with mold. She steps carefully over the shards of mismatched dishware littering the ground, her heart breaking at the unnerving scene.

Without a word, Juniper swallows hard and makes her way down the hallway to the small room she shared with her foster sisters, two year-old Poppy and eight-month old Rosie. She is not surprised to see the crib turned on its side, but the sight of Rosie's well-worn blanket torn nearly in half makes her eyes sting. Poppy's beloved stuffed wolf has also been ripped open and cast aside. She carefully picks it up from the floor to assess whether or not it can be salvaged.

"I've always found it odd they make cute, cuddly versions of ferocious wolves to help the kids sleep at night," Jasper comments, looking over her shoulder.

"At least it's not a bear," Juniper says a little louder than necessary, wondering if it's true what she's heard—that grizzly bears have excellent hearing.

"Hmmmph," Flint makes a loud, disgruntled snort outside, somewhere beneath the tree.

A laugh starts in Juniper's throat, but it is quickly stifled by a hard lump of emotion. A wave of sadness and remorse washes over her, and she hugs Poppy's wolf to her chest. "I should have been here," Juniper says, a tear escaping when her eyes squeeze shut.

"Oh, my dear," Hickory says, placing a heavy hand on her shoulder. "What's broken can be mended. It will just take a little bit of time and—" He is interrupted by a great crash from the next room.

Hickory, Juniper, and Jasper exchange wide-eyed looks. Hickory motions for them to quietly follow him down the hall. Jasper and Juniper crouch behind their uncle's massive form and move forward on the balls of their feet. Juniper remembers the last time she'd crept past the boys' room, sidestepping the creaky floorboards in a similar manner. It was the night she'd discovered her mother's letters and ran away from Foster Hollow. While it couldn't have been more than a few weeks ago, it felt like ages. So much has happened since then.

Juniper can hear her own heart pounding in her ears as Hickory disappears into the boys' room, his slingbow at the ready. Jasper already has an arrow knocked in his bow. Juniper jolts with fear, reaching for her slingshot when she hears her uncle gasp in surprise. After a few moments of heavy silence, Hickory pokes his head around the doorframe with a grin, gesturing it's okay for them to come inside.

Juniper enters the room behind her brother and sighs with relief when she sees the source of the incredible racket. Three trembling chickadee fledglings are huddled together in the top bunk. They had accidentally knocked the toy sword Birch often sleeps with onto the wooden floor with a loud clatter.

"Life continues in the Dark Forest," Hickory marvels aloud.

"Sorrel will be happy to know her home is still a

haven for creatures who need it," Juniper says, smiling widely.

Despite the babies' obvious fear of the unexpected visitors, they appear well-nourished and cared for. "Their mother will likely return soon," Hickory speaks softly. "We should get a move on." Ensuring they mean no harm to the fledglings, the squirrels quietly make their way to Sorrel's room.

"We'll have to work on our room-sweeping technique," Jasper mutters under his breath. Juniper shivers at the thought of what else—or who—might be hiding in the Hollow.

Hickory pushes the door open, and Juniper steps back in surprise. The bookshelves lining the walls are bare, and the floor is a stormy sea of cardboard bits, tattered cloth, and discolored paper.

"What is all of this?" Jasper asks, nudging a pile of scattered documents with his left foot.

"Sorrel's books and letters... they're ruined... " Of all the horrors Juniper has seen today, this feels the most hateful. The weasels had deliberately destroyed the few material belongings Sorrel cherished as her own.

"Why did they do this?" Juniper asks quietly, feeling dazed. Her voice sounds far away.

Hickory clears his throat, choking back tears. "Few know this. Sorrel is a correspondent for the cause. It's complicated, dangerous work." Hickory puts a firm hand on Juniper's. "That's how she was able to receive letters from your mother for all those years. She never knew where to find her, but she had the network to stay connected."

Somehow, this revelation does not surprise Juniper. Sorrel always had a quill tucked into the fur between her ears, scribbling notes, writing letters, and journaling every chance she got. She was never without a book or scrap of paper in her apron pocket. Sorrel would be crushed to see the state of her room now.

"Could the weasels have uncovered something we don't want them to know?" Jasper asks.

"Sorrel has a system. She wouldn't just leave confidential information lying around," Hickory assures him. "More than likely, these books and letters are all meaningful to her in a personal way, but they're inconsequential to the predators."

"They weren't just looking for me," Juniper says out loud, wiping her cheeks with the backs of her paws. "They were looking for something..." She turns to look at Hickory, raising her eyebrows. "The dagger?"

Hickory scratches his head with the feathery end of the arrow he'd been ready to launch from his slingbow. "How would they have known? Jasper sent it only that mornin'."

Juniper stops to think. "Jasper, you said I go

against everything Alder stands for, or something like that... What did you mean? Why is he hunting me? Why *me*?"

Without missing a beat, Jasper replies in a mysterious voice. "'A *young red squirrel bearing the Dagger of Mirren will save us all.*'"

Juniper looks from Jasper to Hickory incredulously. "You really think I'm the one the owl was talking about?"

"Who else? You're the one Aspen left the dagger to..." Jasper shrugs. Juniper can't be sure, but for a moment she thinks she sees a flash of jealousy in his expression.

"Jasper's right," Hickory says quietly.

"But *you're* the one with all the military training," she challenges her brother. "I spent my life *here*... in these tiny rooms. Reading books, babysitting, learning how to cook acorn casserole..."

A stomach rumbles. Jasper and Juniper look at Hickory. "Sorry," he says, his cheeks flushing. "Just mention Sorrel's cooking, and my stomach betrays me."

"I don't want this," Juniper continues, ignoring the interruption. "I didn't ask to be part of some crazy prophecy. How can I fight the evils of this world with just this old, wooden dagger?"

"You don't get to choose the responsibilities you're born with—" Hickory begins, but Juniper cuts him off.

"Let me guess. It's what I *choose* to do with the responsibility that matters," Juniper rattles off, rolling her eyes. "You've spent too much time with Sorrel," she says, feeling conflicting twinges of guilt and satisfaction when she sees the sorrowful look on Hickory's face. Being back in Foster Hollow, witnessing its destruction, and feeling the pressure of an outrageous prophecy hanging over her head has her emotions in shambles. Her sass is short-lived, however, when a distant howl reminds them dusk is quickly approaching.

"Time to go," Jasper sighs. "We have to get back to the Bramble by nightfall."

TWO
FLASH OF RED

In the daytime, The Dark Forest isn't as menacing as its name suggests. Shafts of yellow sunlight filter through thick evergreen branches, heavy with pinecones. Despite Flint's lumbering steps, he pads softly over a cool carpet of moss and pine needles. Juniper has lived here her entire life, but she is just coming to learn the woods' designation is more of a warning than a description.

"In the midst of the Unraveling, a small number of creatures that survived the great flood decided to stay rather than escape to nearby islands," Hickory explains. "Many of them had no choice—they weren't able to swim or fly like the others. Some found safe places to live in abandoned nests and burrows here in the Dark Forest."

"Like Sorrel," Juniper adds.

"Like Sorrel," Hickory nods. "The river on this side of the mountains ran to a trickle and eventually went dry, but these resourceful animals found ways to survive on the outskirts of predator territory.

Guardians were appointed to protect the Forest. Together, we've been able to take the few predators that dare to prowl before sunset. Their senses are slower and weaker in the daylight. The curfew is meant to keep all creatures in doors when darkness falls—that's when the wolves and coyotes prefer to do their hunting."

The implication of Hickory's words hang heavy in the air. *They hunt creatures like us.* Juniper's stomach lurches as she remembers the conversation she'd had with Jasper before they'd set out for Foster Hollow at daybreak. *"Before we go, I have something to tell you,"* he'd said. *"It's our father... We've received word of where he might be held prisoner."* To keep herself focused on the day's dangerous journey, Juniper had done her best to push Jasper's startling news to the far corners of her mind. Now, her heart leaps with a second surge of hope. *Was that only this morning? Our father might be out there somewhere... is it possible that the predators have kept him alive all this time?*

Juniper shifts uncomfortably on Flint's back and does her best to shake the exciting yet troubling thoughts from her mind once again. Her knapsack hangs heavy on her shoulders, lumpy with her foster siblings' belongings. Before they'd left the Hollow, she had gone back through the rooms to retrieve Rosie's blanket, Poppy's stuffed wolf, and Birch's toy sword, adding them to the small pile of Dougie's blocks she'd collected. She plans to surprise them by mending their beloved items, which will surely bring smiles to their sweet faces.

"We haven't seen a single guardian all day." Hickory interrupts Juniper's hopeful daydream with a hint of worry in his voice. "This is Elm's territory. He should be making his rounds right about now, calling for curfew."

"It's too quiet," Jasper agrees. "Something's not right."

"Can we stop here for a moment, Flint?" Hickory asks. "I'd like to check in on a fellow soldier."

"Make it quick," Flint grumbles. "The sun will be setting soon."

A strange feeling rises in Juniper's stomach. She watches Jasper slip down Flint's back with ease and follow Hickory into what appears to be a small, inconspicuous ground squirrel hole a few yards away. She attempts to push the queasiness away by distracting herself with conversation. "Flint, may I ask you something?"

"Like what?"

"Are there any of your kind left?" The day's adventures have left Juniper feeling bold and full of questions. Juniper can't be sure, but she thinks she feels Flint wince beneath his thick, black fur.

"I hope so," he says. "There used to be a great

many of us."

"What happened?"

After a quiet moment, Flint clears his throat. "The wolves and coyotes joined forces against us. The predators greatly outnumbered us. We fought ferociously, but there were simply too many of them."

"But, you're so much bigger than they are." Juniper frowns, trying to picture a pack of wolves and coyotes taking on a sleuth of grizzly bears.

"It's sheer statistics, kid. Twenty of them to one of us. It's likely worse now." Flint pauses and sinks down to the ground with a heavy thump. He rests his head on his front paws and releases a long, deep sigh before continuing. Juniper grabs a handful of coarse fur to keep from toppling to the forest floor. "We had to do what was safe for our children. I'd made an oath to protect the Alliance and guard Mirren with my life. I stayed behind. The rest swam for safety."

Juniper's throat swells with sadness.

"My daughter was carrying her first cub when she crossed Dogwood Bay," Flint continues. "I believe I have a granddaughter or grandson just about your age out there somewhere."

A tear slides down Juniper's cheek. She is struck by the revelation that loss and grief are a part of the greater story—not just her own. Her heart aches for Flint.

"Why haven't you gone to find them?"

"I—" Flint begins, but his body goes rigid before he can finish his story. His great nose sniffs the air and his right ear twitches.

"Don't. Move."

Before Juniper detects any sign of danger in the nearby foliage, a flash of rust-colored fur bursts into the clearing, bounding toward them like a leaping flame.

Flint rises to his feet without warning, and Juniper is thrown from her perch on his back. She gathers her bearings on a patch of moss before scurrying up the nearest tree. She trembles on a nearby branch, watching the fox circle the grizzly bear with bared teeth.

Juniper squints at the copper creature that looks so much like her brother's best friend and fellow soldier.

It's not Sitka. It can't be.

The closer she looks, the more convinced she is right. This canine is leaner. The outlines of its ribs are visible each time it pants. And yet—this creature's resemblance to Sitka is uncanny. A shiver runs down her spine.

Just when Juniper finds herself wondering if the standoff will ever end, the fox makes its move, lunging for Flint's throat. Flint knocks the fox to the ground with one great swipe of his paw. The predator lets out a howl of pain. Juniper covers her mouth when a flash of red darkens a fresh, gaping tear in its left ear.

A moment later, the familiar clunking of wooden armor announces Hickory and Jasper's return. The fox vanishes into the brush just as Hickory reappears from the ground squirrel hole.

Hickory takes one look at Flint and Juniper, and his face drops. "What happened?"

"A fox attacked us," Juniper takes a shaky breath.

"But we're fine. I sent it runnin'," Flint says.

"See anything suspicious?" Juniper asks, quickly wiping her face with the back of her paw, eager to move on. She notices Hickory is carrying a small, triangular piece of wood adorned with a cursive "G"—the mark of the guardian.

"Somethin'... which might be nothin'," Hickory says with concern, his eyes scanning the perimeter for any sign of red fur. He is clearly disturbed by the news of the attack. "I found Elm's badge. He may have abandoned his post—or worse."

THREE
BITTER BLACKBERRIES

The grizzly bear and his small companions arrive safely at the Bramble just in time for supper. Still rattled from the fox attack, Flint keeps watch while Juniper, Jasper, and Hickory disappear into the tunnel entrance hidden beneath a snarl of thorny blackberry vines. When he hears the stone door grind shut, Flint turns to enter through his own secret passage.

Juniper parts ways with Hickory and Jasper at the entrance to the Great Hall. Despite its grand name, it is little more than a long tent furnished with rows of oak tables and benches. "I'm going to find Sorrel," she calls over her shoulder, leaving Jasper and Hickory to fall in line behind a string of hungry, young soldiers waiting for the serving line to open.

Juniper enters the steamy kitchen pavilion to find Sorrel stirring a large pot of pine nut stew with a frown on her face and baby Rosie clinging to her hip. Her foster mother had quickly found a way to use her passions and skills to serve at Logan Bramble.

"June," Sorrel's eyes widen with relief when they

land on Juniper. "You're back later than I expected. I was getting worried. How'd it go?"

Not wanting to frighten little ears that might be listening, Juniper shakes her head, and Sorrel frowns. "We'll talk later," she whispers, nodding towards the children scurrying about the kitchen. "Supper's ready, everyone!"

Juniper smiles, watching the older foster children's faces while helping serve the Archers' evening meal. Fern, the most recent arrival, squeals with delight when he is given the task of passing out chestnut biscuits. Even little Poppy is excited to help, running back and forth between the kitchen and serving lines to deliver small handfuls of napkins and forks. The children's wide eyes sparkle in awe and admiration as the weary soldiers hold out empty plates to receive their food.

When most of the troops have been served, Juniper follows Sorrel to a long table at the far end of the great hall. They have been invited to dine with the general tonight. She smiles when she sees her uncles, Hemlock and Hickory, her brother, Jasper, and her friends, Willow and Rhodie, are already seated. There's only one creature missing. Juniper frowns.

"Where's Sitka?" she asks her brother.

"He's on guard duty," Jasper mumbles from the side of his mouth, already chomping on a chestnut biscuit.

A loud knocking sound distracts Juniper from her inquiry. She turns toward the head of the table where General Hemlock is seated. In the space next to him, where there is room for one more, a pair of young soldiers struggle to open a pair of heavy wooden doors hidden in the ground.

When the hatch is finally lifted, the grizzly bear's burly black head pokes through. "Ah, Flint," the General nods. "I'm glad you could join us."

In the days following Flint's arrival, Sorrel had persuaded General Hemlock to arrange for a team of burrowing moles, ground squirrels, and rabbits to engineer a secure, separate entryway out of respect for the last-known living member of the First Alliance. Now, he has a secure underground den to rest comfortably in and long, wide tunnels to give him access to various places around the military installation.

While Flint is too large to enter the training grounds the traditional way, he is still able to have a place at the table and participate in important conversations. At least, his large, intimidating *head* is.

Just out of Flint's range of vision, Jasper attempts to make the kids giggle by ducking under the table and slowly raising his face so only his ears, eyes, and the tip of his nose are visible. When he's sure the children are looking, he snatches a bite of food from his plate without using his paws and chomps wildly, imitating Flint's awkward dining arrangement. Juniper nearly chokes on a sip of dandelion nectar, and Hickory shoots a stern look at the two of them before cracking a smile himself. It feels good to laugh.

"Now," General Hemlock clears his throat. "Let us toast to the safe return of Flint, my brother, and my niece and nephew."

Glasses brimming with nectar are raised and lowered as the meal begins. Jasper volunteers to share an abridged version of the day's events between bites of pine nut stew, mushroom tart, and chestnut biscuits. Although fungus is not her favorite, Juniper eats more than her fill of each dish. Just when she feels as though she can't force another bite of food down her throat, a young rabbit brings a tray with servings of blackberry shortcake on tiny plates.

"I'm not going to be able to squeeze into my armor after this meal, and I'm okay with that," Rhodie sighs in satisfaction, and Willow giggles.

After ensuring each of the children enjoyed a helping of dessert, Sorrel excuses herself to escort them off to their tents for the night. Having become quite fond of Juniper's foster siblings, Rhodie and Willow offer to help Sorrel with the bedtime routine. Juniper puts down her napkin to follow suit, but her foster mother stops her.

"Stay and have an extra bite of cake, June."

Sorrel squeezes her shoulder. "You've had a long day."

Once again, Juniper remembers the startling information Jasper had shared with her when they'd set out on their journey at daylight. *Our father might be alive.* She has to swallow hard to push a mouthful of blackberries down her throat. *Why aren't we addressing this news?*

When Sorrel returns a short time later, Hickory pushes back his plate.

"Now that the children have gone to bed, there's something I need to tell you, Sorrel." Sorrel's shoulders fall with worry, but Hickory is quick to reassure her. "Don't fret, darlin'—it's good news. Fern's father has been located. He's alive. As soon as we make sure it's absolutely safe for the boy, he can return home."

This is news to Juniper—and Jasper too, apparently. Instinctively, her eyes land on her brother's face to gauge his reaction. He looks just as surprised as Juniper feels. Hickory hadn't spoken a word about *their father*, let alone Fern or his family all day.

Little Fern had been the newest arrival at Foster Hollow. Hickory had placed him in Sorrel's care on the evening of Juniper's birthday—the night she'd chosen to run away. Awful visions of the tattered books and scattered letters that now litter Sorrel's bedroom floor flood her memory.

"Oh, that's wonderful," Sorrel sighs, her smile of relief contrasting the twist of shame in Juniper's stomach. Her foster mother closes her eyes and lets out a deep breath. "It's been so long since we've been able to reunite a family."

Over the years, it has happened more times than Juniper can count. She has watched young squirrels come, blossom in varying degrees in Sorrel's care, and then return to their families. Each time, Juniper wonders if it might be her turn next. While Juniper is genuinely happy for Fern, a sharp, familiar stitch of jealousy and longing tugs at her chest.

"What about his mother? And, I believe he has an older sister, too." Sorrel asks.

Flint shakes his head sadly. "Still missing. Their father said a fox attacked in broad daylight."

After a moment of sickened silence, Jasper speaks up on his friend's behalf. "There hasn't been another fox on this side of the Waste since Sitka arrived at the Bramble," Jasper furrows his brow.

"We know, son," Hemlock lets out a tired sigh.

"But—he wouldn't hurt a field mouse," Jasper defends his friend. "No offense, Rhodie."

Rhodie shrugs. "None taken," she says, smiling. A shower of shortcake crumbs falls from her whiskers.

"We think it might be his brother, Spruce. Fern's father described a younger fox."

"Could it be the same one we crossed today?" Hickory looks at Flint.

"It's very likely—next time, we'll be able to recognize him. He'll have a piece of his ear missin'." The grizzly bear grumbles.

"Can we talk about *our* father, now?" Jasper asks, speaking Juniper's thoughts out loud with an unusual edge to his voice. Juniper catches a glimpse of Hemlock and Hickory exchanging looks of concern.

"We need time to investigate the information Sergeant Sitka has collected," Hemlock spoke as the general, not Jasper's uncle.

"What information?" Juniper asks, her wide, green eyes flitting between her uncles and brother. Their unspoken tension made the fur on the back of her neck stand up.

"I'm afraid it's classified, my dear," Hemlock says, taking a long, final sip of dandelion nectar from his wooden cup as if to put an end to the discussion.

Juniper frowns. *Great. More secrets.*

"General, I assure you Sitka is trustworthy," Jasper continues. "We can send out a team as early as tomorrow—"

"You will follow my orders, Captain." Hemlock's expression hardens. "We will not discuss this further."

Juniper notices Jasper's bottom lip is trembling with emotion. He is clearly upset to be arguing with his uncle and superior officer. "I'm sick of waiting around for orders," he blurts out. "This is the first scrap of information we've gotten in years. Our father could be dying out there!"

"And it could be a trap," Hemlock responds, his tone shifting with warning. "He might be dead already."

Jasper stands and bangs his fists on the table, knocking over an empty cup.

"Who's side are you on? You act like you've given up on him! Your own brother!"

General Hemlock appears to grow twice his size when he pushes his own chair back from the table and glowers at his nephew. "Remember your rank, soldier," he barks.

Jasper clenches his jaw and swallows hard. "Yes. Sir."

Juniper cringes when her brother gives their uncle a patronizing salute. The temperature inside the tent seems to have dropped quickly. Juniper shivers at the sudden chill in the air.

Hemlock breaks the icy silence with a great sigh. "I know you're anxious, Jasper," he says. "I am, too. We all are. After all these years, we're desperate to find our brother. Your father. But we have to remain logical and strategic." His tone is firm and final. "The New Alliance is counting on us."

Juniper expects her brother to regain his composure and continue to protest in his typical charismatic yet annoying manner. Instead, he swallows hard, bites his bottom lip, and tosses his napkin onto his plate.

Jasper clears his throat. "Good night, everyone. Thank you for another wonderful supper, Sorrel. It was scrumptious—as usual."

Juniper watches her brother dust the crumbs from his lap and force a respectful salute before he leaves the table. She takes one last bite of blackberry shortcake, and it suddenly tastes bitter on her tongue.

FOUR
THE WARBLERS

The candle's flame flickers over the last passage Juniper and Sorrel had read together in the Book of Mirren the night before. Since Sorrel had given Juniper her own copy of the Book—even after she'd stolen it from her foster mother's night stand—she has been reading the old text with a new perspective. She hungers to find meaning behind the puzzling words and stories that tell of the Unraveling and what Mirren was like before it fell. The passages are repetitious and difficult to comprehend, but with Sorrel's guidance, the more Juniper reads, the more she understands. She has come to look forward to these after-dinner lessons and conversations. Not to mention, being able to accept visitors in her own tent makes her feel more grown up.

Juniper's thoughts scatter when Sorrel's face pushes through the tent flap. She looks more weary and gray-haired than usual.

"I brought you a cup of daisy petal tea." Sorrel offers a tired smile along with the thoughtful treat.

"Thank you." Juniper accepts the drink and warms her hands on the wooden cup.

"Now, tell me," Sorrel says, sitting on the edge of Juniper's cot. "What happened today? I've heard Jasper's version, but I'd like to hear yours."

Juniper is prepared to recount the day's events slowly and with as little emotion as possible, but she throws her arms around her foster mother instead. "It's awful, Sorrel. Doors are ripped from their hinges. Dishes are broken. Every room is torn apart—yours, especially. I don't know how we'll ever manage to repair the damage."

Juniper draws back from Sorrel's shoulder to gauge her expression. When she sees the deep sadness in her eyes, she loosens her embrace and attempts to lighten the mood.

"Something kind of funny happened, though." The corner of Juniper's mouth lifts in a half-smile. "There was this loud crash in the boys' room. For a moment, I was afraid it might be a weasel lurking around, but Hickory investigated, and he found a nest of chickadees in the top bunk! They'd accidentally knocked Birch's sword to the floor. Oh! That reminds me."

Juniper turns to retrieve her knapsack. "I brought it back for him." She reveals the wooden sword and dumps the rest of the gifts onto her cot for Sorrel to see. "I retrieved these for the others, too."

Sorrel's eyes swim with emotion above her weary smile. "They will like that very much." Juniper can't remember her foster mother ever looking so frail.

"I'm so glad you're alright, my dear," Sorrel sighs. "You did something brave today, so I figured I could too. I finally had the nerve to wash the clothes we were wearing the night the weasels attacked Foster Hollow. I hadn't even gone through them yet—for a while, it bothered me too much to look at them." She nervously smooths her wrinkled blue smock with her paws. "I found this in my apron pocket," she says, handing a crinkled envelope to Juniper. "It arrived on your birthday. In the midst of the chaos of that night, I forgot all about it. I'm so sorry it's taken me so long to give it to you. Can you please forgive me—again?"

Juniper sits in stunned silence for a moment, her eyes fixed on the tattered envelope. Finally, she nods her head and accepts the letter from Sorrel's extended paw.

She swallows hard. The paper feels hot in her hands. By her own calculations, one letter from her mother had arrived every year on her birthday until she'd turned eleven; after that, the messages had ceased. This was the first note to have been sent in three years—and the first Sorrel has ever delivered herself.

"Will you stay here with me while I open it?"

Sorrel nods. The sound of ripping paper seems louder than it should be as Juniper tears open the envelope and unfolds the note. Her mother's familiar loopy letters appear to tangle together on the page, as if they had been written in a hurry.

Dear Juniper,

Please forgive me for how long it's been since I've written. Not a day goes by that I don't wish we could be together. I have much to say, but I'm risking everything to get this news to you. Your father is alive. You will receive word of this soon, if you haven't already. I will write again when I can. Tell Sorrel I miss her dearly.

All my love,
Mom

Juniper's eyes sting with a mixture of tears and exhaustion, and her mother's handwriting blurs until she can only see two sentences clearly:

I'm risking everything to get this news to you. Your father is alive...

Simultaneous rushes of fear and relief make her stomach tremble.

What trouble could her mother be in? And, how could she know her father is alive?

After a moment, the buzz of shock settles to a dull hum in her head. Remembering the last words her mother scribbled before closing the letter, she looks up at Sorrel's concerned face.

Tell Sorrel I miss her dearly, she'd said.

"How do you know my mom?"

Sorrel smiles warmly, but Juniper notices the corners of her mouth are trembling. Sorrel swallows hard. "We grew up together."

"You were friends?"

"More like sisters."

Juniper furrows her eyebrows.

"Before the Unraveling..." Sorrel pauses as if she isn't sure how to go on. "Before the Unraveling, my family's nest was attacked in an early predator uprising. I was just a kit, then. I hardly remember anything. The Warbler's—Laurel's parents, *your* grandparents—took me in and raised me as their own. Laurel was just a wee one, then." She reaches into her pocket and draws out a second envelope. This one is yellow, faded, and already torn open. "I have something else for you."

Juniper takes the note from Sorrel's hand and reads it aloud.

My dear sister Sorrel,

The time has come for me to make an impossible decision. I hope you understand this is the only choice I have. Please take Juniper and keep her safe—

At the sound of her own name, Juniper's breath catches in her throat. She has to swallow an aching lump to continue.

Jasper is with Hemlock. I don't want to separate my children but I know I have to—for their safety. We must keep the stones apart as long as we can.

Love Juniper like your own daughter. Raise her to love the Book and overcome—just as you do. I know you will. I hope to hug you both again one day.

Until then and with all my heart,
Your sister, L

"So you see," Sorrel squeezes Juniper's paw.

"Laurel and I were raised as sisters. This note was left on my doorstep, along with the most precious baby girl I'd ever seen." She smiles sadly. "I carry it with me to remind me of why we're doing all this—what's most important—when I forget."

Juniper's tongue feels heavy, and she realizes her paws are trembling. It takes a little longer than it should to carefully fold the letter along the old creases and return it to its crumpled envelope.

"For a while, I didn't know where Jasper was..." Juniper hears Sorrel continuing, and it sounds as if she's in a different room. "When I learned he was in Hemlock's care, a piece of me felt it was wrong to keep you apart. At the same time, Hickory urged me to follow your mother's instructions. I was willing to do whatever I had to do to keep you both safe. As your mother said, it was an impossible decision."

Juniper reaches up to touch the smooth hunk of amber dangling from her neck. *We must keep the stones apart as long as we can.* What does this mean?

"Why haven't you told me any of this?"

"Keeping secrets is my job," Sorrel sighs. "Sometimes I have a difficult time knowing when to keep quiet and when it's safe to talk."

Juniper studies her paws in silence for a moment. "Are there any other secrets I should know about? What about... Hickory?"

"What do you mean?"

"I see the way you are with each other. He calls you *darlin'*." Juniper can't help but giggle.

Sorrel smiles, warmth rising to her cheeks. "I keep forgetting how mature you are for your age. It's true, I love Hickory... but, sometimes, there are things more important than romance." Sorrel folds her hands in her lap with finality and quickly attempts to circle back to the matter at hand. "How are you feeling—about everything?"

"I'm..." Juniper tries to name the emotions swirling around in her chest, but the words won't come. "I don't know. It's hard to explain. It hurts to think about not getting to grow up with my mom and dad. Jasper, too. I've missed so much. I'm grateful to have you... and, I'm also sad and angry—about being left behind, I guess." Juniper's voice trembles with conflicting feelings of relief and guilt. "I'm confused."

She buries her head in her paws, afraid to look up at Sorrel. She doesn't want to see the pain her honesty must have caused on her foster mother's face. Warm tears run down Juniper's cheeks, and her face burns with shame.

After a moment of heavy silence, Juniper feels Sorrel's paw on her shoulder. She squeezes gently. "I understand," Sorrel speaks quietly. "I often feel the same way."

Surprised, Juniper lowers her paws to find empathy and compassion rather than anger and offense in Sorrel's eyes. "You do?"

Sorrel nods. "Love is complicated... and sometimes very painful. Often, the best choice is also the hardest."

Juniper chews on Sorrel's mysterious words for a moment. When she feels another lump threatening to replace the last, Juniper offers to change the course of the conversation, eager to focus on something other than her own perplexing emotions.

"Are you ready to read?"

"Yes," Sorrel smiles, folding her paws in her lap. "Now, where were we?"

Juniper clears her throat, dries her eyes with the soft fur on the back of her paw, and pulls the Book of Mirren into her lap. Feeling for the feather she'd tucked between the pages, she finds the paragraph where they'd left off the night before.

"In the beginning, every creature of Mirren was given special skills to use for the good of all..."

FIVE

SMOKE

Juniper wakes with the words Sorrel had spoken over her when she'd said good night echoing in her thoughts. *Creator, thank you for precious Juniper. Please watch over her, protect her, and help her know how much she is loved...*

Her mind still foggy with sleep, she realizes there was a time not long ago when Sorrel's prayers had melted into the softness and comfort of her childhood bedtime routine. With a kiss on the forehead and a tuck into warm blankets, they tumbled off Sorrel's lips like sweet lullaby lyrics and nothing more. Now, the words feel heavier. Sharper. She wants to know more about this Creator Sorrel speaks to.

Juniper opens her eyes and lifts her head from the pages of the Book. She'd fallen asleep at her desk, continuing to read long after Sorrel had said goodnight. Pressed daisy petals cling to the bottom of her overturned tea cup. Assessing the height of the candle she'd left burning, she guesses it's not quite midnight. Juniper yawns and moves to shut her book, but the words on the page swirl together. Looking around the tent, she notices her surroundings appear hazy.

For one confused moment, Juniper thinks she's still dreaming. Blinking hard, Juniper tries to clear her eyes. She spots a curl of smoke rising from the tent flap. Sooty fumes irritate her throat, and she begins to cough.

Something's wrong.

Juniper dashes out of the tent to find Logan Bramble in a state of chaos. Flames flicker wildly on the edge of her vision while she takes in the scene unfolding before her. With wide eyes, she watches a pair of moles rush with stretchers carrying soldiers wrapped in red-tinged bandages. At the sight of wooden medic badges hanging from cords around the moles' necks, she springs into action. Ducking back into her tent, she quickly gathers the necessities. Armor. Slingshot. Dagger.

Sorrel. The kids. I have to get to them.

Juniper strides to the next row of tents, where Poppy, Rosie, and Sorrel are staying until they are able to return to Foster Hollow. She pushes her head through each opening, her eyes sweeping quickly over piles of disheveled bedding. *They should all be asleep at this time of night. Where are they?* She moves on to the boys' tent and finds a similarly unnerving scene. Panic rises in her chest when she catches sight of a familiar copper tail.

"Sitka! What's going on?" She calls, her voice scratchy.

"Get to the Great Hall! Flint will go through the evacuation procedures!"

Evacuation procedures?

Before Juniper can ask follow up questions, the fox disappears in the haze. She races forward blindly, trusting her instincts will lead her where she needs to go. With every heavy pound of her heart, another frantic thought crosses her mind.

What's happening? Are the children safe? Where will we go?

"Ouch!" Juniper stumbles into an archery target and realizes she's gotten turned around in the smoke. Rubbing her elbow, she notices a familiar form lying still on the ground a short distance away. Panic rises in her throat when she comes close enough to make out the features of her brother's face.

"Jasper! What happened? Are you okay?"

Jasper groans in response, and she spots a long, crimson gash on his upper arm.

"Medic!" she calls. "Medic?" A small rabbit appears at her side with a bag of medical supplies.

"He'll be fine," the rabbit says, working quickly. "Just a surface wound."

Juniper's attention shifts to a struggling pair of

shadowy figures, one towering over the other, a few yards ahead. Through the smoke, the larger creature appears to have the smaller by the nape of its neck, while its arms and legs swing wildly in the air.

"Lemme go!" The small animal shouts as it attempts to kick and throw punches at its captor, fighting back. Juniper recognizes Birch's voice, and her heart drops into her stomach.

Without thinking, she reaches for her slingshot and fits a pebble into its leather strap.

"Birch!" She shouts as the small rock releases and connects with the jaw of the larger figure. It slumps to the ground unconscious, releasing its grip on her tiny foster brother. Juniper sprints to his aid as the figure on the ground nearby moans in pain. She gasps when she recognizes Birch's captor.

"Uncle Hickory!"

"Way to go, Hotshot," Jasper's voice calls in a light, almost comical tone. "You just got one of the good guys."

Like waking from a nightmare, Juniper's surroundings begin to soften and take shape before her. Juniper blinks, and her brother's face comes into focus. Before she can ask how he managed to recover so quickly, he begins to laugh.

"You do know this is a drill, right?"

"What? A... a drill?" Juniper turns and takes in the scene as if seeing it for the first time. The shock of smoke and fire in the Bramble kept her from noticing the irregular rock formations circling the flames. She can now see rectangular fire pits strategically placed around the Bramble to give the illusion of an attack. *The burning is controlled.* Juniper lets out a long, shaky breath, and her cheeks burn with embarrassment.

Juniper shakes her head in disbelief while Jasper bends down to rouse Hickory awake where he'd fallen. "I'm so sorry, Hickory..." she begins to apologize, her voice trembling.

"Ah, I'm fine, Juniper," Hickory mumbles in assurance, but his wince tells her otherwise. "I'm glad you're making good use of the slingshot I gave you." She watches as he rises, turns, and disappears into the nearest tent, pressing his paw to the tender spot where the pebble had collided with his jaw. She is surprised to discover they are standing in front of the Great Hall.

"Juniper, your chestplate is on backwards," Jasper comments, looking puzzled. "How did you even manage to get it on that way? That's very impressive..."

"Jasper!" Juniper thumps her brother on the chest, the initial flash of anger cooling with a rush of relief. "Why didn't you tell me we were having a drill?!"

"It wouldn't have been a true exercise if I had,

now would it? And, it would have spoiled all the fun," Jasper raises his eyebrows playfully.

"It all looked—felt—so real." Juniper's mind is still spinning.

"Good," Jasper says. "It was supposed to."

"The blood..." Juniper says, shaking her head in disbelief.

"It's fake. The ingredients are similar to Sorrel's strawberry syrup." Jasper winks, running the tip of his paw along the edge of his bandage where a bit of red liquid is oozing out. He pops it in his mouth. "Mmm. Delicious."

Juniper scoffs.

"What about Birch? I thought Hickory was a predator trying to take him..."

"Birch wanted to come find you, and Hickory was trying to get him to join the other kids in the Great Hall for a midnight snack."

Juniper ducks beneath the large canopy to see Birch, Dougie, Poppy, and Fern seated at a nearby table. All are nibbling sleepily on warm hazelnut cookies while Rosie dozes peacefully on Sorrel's shoulder.

Tears of relief spring to Juniper's eyes.

"If it makes you feel any better—you passed. As long as we don't count that run-in with Hickory." Jasper winks. "The general wants to see you, now."

SIX
HEMLOCK'S REQUEST

I passed? Passed what?

Juniper's heart is still racing from what she'd thought had been an attack on the Bramble. She enters the general's intimidating tent with slumped shoulders to find her uncle calmly studying worn, paper maps sprawled across his large desk. He looks up at her over round spectacles sitting on his nose.

"Is this about Hickory? I feel awful," Juniper chatters nervously. "I was confused. I didn't know about the drill, and I thought he was a predator of some kind, meaning to hurt Birch—"

Hemlock raises a paw and grins. "My brother's fine. He's been through far worse, I assure you."

"I'm sorry I hurt him." Juniper looks down at her feet, her stomach swimming with guilt.

"You have a true soldier's spirit, Juniper. Fierce yet compassionate. You put others before yourself today." Hemlock removes his reading glasses and places them on the map in front of him. "What's your plan for the future?"

"My plan?" Juniper's eyes drop to her feet. "There's a lot that must be done to make Foster Hollow liveable again. I plan to return with Sorrel as soon as we're able." It's been so long, Juniper realizes she actually misses her daily chore of collecting rainwater pouches. She aches to be on her own for a short while, free to think and daydream in the calm and quiet of the Forest before curfew.

"What would you say if I asked you to consider staying here to learn the ways of the Archers?" Hemlock asks. "We need more soldiers like you, Juniper. I have reason to believe another great war is on the horizon, and we need all the help we can get when—not if—the predators attack. I've spoken with Jasper, and he agrees to oversee your training."

Juniper is stunned. It's no secret she has been jealous of Jasper for growing up with Hemlock and attending Bramble Academy, the school for prospective Archers. Now, she doesn't know what to say. A moment of uncomfortable silence passes before she gathers the courage to ask the question that's been on her mind since she arrived at Logan Bramble.

"Why didn't I grow up here? Like Jasper?"

Hemlock had an answer ready on his lips, as if he knew she'd ask. "Quite frankly, it's because you needed more protection."

"Because I'm a girl?"

HEMLOCK'S REQUEST

Hemlock smiles. "Because you had to be hidden. Logan Bramble is no secret. Lord Alder has known exactly where Jasper's been all this time. He's not the one Alder's after."

"Lord Alder is your father."

"Yes, and *your* grandfather. He's a very dangerous squirrel. You are of great interest to him."

"Because of the prophecy?"

Hemlock nods.

"But, I thought the old owl is supposed to be crazy?"

"Let's call her by her name, shall we? Oleander is a bit eccentric." Hemlock chuckles. "But, she's also very wise. I think wisdom has a way of making you appear a little nutty to those who don't understand."

Juniper searches Hemlock's expression for any sign of humor and finds none.

"What about you? What do you think?" Juniper challenges her uncle.

"It doesn't matter what I think. It matters what Lord Alder thinks."

For a moment, Juniper considers mentioning the note from her mother. *My father is alive.* Before she opens her mouth, she remembers the awkward moment between Jasper, Hemlock, and Hickory at the dinner table, and she decides to keep it to herself.

"Can I take some time to think about your request?" Juniper asks. "I'd like to talk to Sorrel."

The general nods. "Of course. A thoughtful response, indeed."

Juniper reaches up to grab the amber stone hanging at the base of her throat when she turns to leave her uncle's tent. Lifting the dagger from its place on her hip, she compares her necklace to the gem embedded in the weapon's hilt. While both stones glow beautifully when held up to the light, there doesn't appear to be anything extraordinary about either of them.

What makes these old lumps of hardened tree sap so significant? Special enough to keep a brother and sister away from one another for years? Important enough to have a grandfather hunt down his own granddaughter?

SEVEN

ABOUT FACE

Juniper bites her lip when the archery range comes into view. The morning air is crisp and cool, but her cheeks and ears are flushed with heat. Half of her is still steaming from the previous night's drill and Jasper's nasty trick; the other wishes Sorrel had forbade Hemlock's proposition—or given a definitive answer one way or the other, not leaving it up to Juniper to decide.

"What do *you* think you should do?" Sorrel returned the question when Juniper asked for advice regarding her uncle's offer. "I can't make this decision for you," she had spoken firmly. "You have to do what *you* believe is right, June."

What choice would my mother make in my position? What would my father encourage me to do?

She spots Jasper's bright orange fur in the line of Archers at the range. Up until the moment she approaches him, she isn't sure what her decision will be. All this time, she's been longing for a sense of purpose, and now... the fur on the back of her neck prickles with fear. *Or is it excitement?*

Blackberry leaves crunch beneath Juniper's feet when she plants herself in front of her brother and crosses her arms. Jasper's bow is raised. He appears focused on his target and unaware of her presence. After a moment of awkward silence, Jasper clears his throat.

"Well?" He raises an eyebrow over an inquisitive frown without breaking his concentration. "Have you made your decision?"

"Yes," she breathes. "I'm on my way to tell Hemlock I've decided..." Juniper squeezes her eyes shut as the words come rushing out. "I'm in."

A wide grin takes over Jasper's serious expression, and his arrow whizzes through the air. It strikes the center of the target on the other side of the field before Juniper can take back her answer.

"Great," he says, clapping his paws together. "Now the fun begins."

Sorrel's intuition had told her a celebratory lunch would be appropriate, or she'd known comfort food should be on the menu regardless. Before Juniper has a chance to rethink her decision, she is seated at the general's table in the Great Hall among her family members and closest friends.

"Congratulations!" Willow squeals, her high-pitched voice twinkling over her buzzing wings.

"We're thrilled to have you join the ranks!" Rhodie squeaks over Willow's hum, giving Juniper a warm hug before settling into the seat to her right. "We've considered you one of us all along, of course. I'm excited for it to be official."

"I'm so proud of you, June." Sorrel beams from her seat across the table. "Your mother and father would be, too."

Juniper's cheeks redden as she looks around the table at the faces now set upon her own. She locks eyes with Sitka, who gives her an approving nod. As usual, she can't read the emotions behind Flint's thick black fur, but she has a feeling he is pleased with her decision. General Hemlock smiles back at her, practically glowing with pride, and Hickory appears to be blinking back tears.

"Where are the kids?" Juniper asks, attempting to steer the conversation away from herself.

"They've been allowed to begin lessons at Bramble Academy." Sorrel grins widely. "Even little Rosie is getting to play with new friends."

This news pleases Juniper. Perhaps an extended stay at Logan Bramble would be a good thing for them after all.

Jasper plunks into the last empty seat on her left, interrupting her thoughts and giving her shoulder an affectionate squeeze. He raises a cup of blackberry cider. "I would like to toast my little sister, who will soon be Lieutenant Spark! I think she has what it takes to make it as an Archer," he says, his expression softening for a moment before cocking his left eyebrow. "You could say it runs in the family."

Jasper basks in the chuckles and eye rolls that pass around the table before he continues. "To you, Juniper," he says, and the sentiment echoes around the Great Hall.

"To Juniper!"

Juniper barely tastes the tangy, purple juice when it passes her lips. She is thankful to see trays of food arrive, turning her loved ones' attention away from her decision and onto their filling plates. When the din of conversation picks up, Juniper leans toward her brother.

"Will you be there for my training?" She asks, pushing honey roasted pine nuts around her plate.

"For some of it," he says, winking over a mouthful of walnut crumble. "The part where the bows and arrows are involved." He takes a long sip of blackberry cider and nods toward her untouched meal. "You better eat what you can now. Enjoy your fill. Barracks food is definitely not as delicious as Sorrel's home cooking."

───✶───

A pair of young rabbits, both officers, arrive when the last of the plates are being cleared. Juniper watches them march across the Great Hall, steps in sync, before coming to a halt at the head of the table where Hemlock is seated. They raise their paws in salute. "General, we're here to accompany Cadet Spark to the barracks," the taller of the two announces.

"Carry on, gentlemen," Hemlock pushes away from the table to stand and turn toward his niece. "Juniper, it's time."

Juniper gives her cloth napkin one last anxious twist before tossing it onto her empty placemat. Sorrel and Hickory make their way around the table to give her tight hugs.

"Tell the kids I love them, and I'll see them soon," Juniper speaks into Sorrel's soft fur. She smells of warm honey and toasted walnuts.

"I will," Sorrel says, pulling away with glistening eyes.

"You're going to do great, kiddo," Hickory says in a scratchy voice, wrapping his heavy arms around her for a brief moment.

"Thanks, Uncle Hickory," she says, fighting a lump in her throat.

Juniper bids farewell to the rest of her friends, and Rhodie and Willow follow Juniper back to her tent, where she is allowed to quickly pack a small bag of necessities. She carefully tucks her slingshot and dagger between an extra tunic and the Book of

Mirren. Juniper's eyes flicker over the stack of her mother's letters sitting on the desk. She makes the decision to bring only one—the letter that had just arrived this week.

"Will you hold on to these for me?" Juniper hands the rest to Rhodie.

"Of course," she nods.

Juniper takes one last look around her comfortable tent—the only space she has ever had to herself—before taking a deep breath and ducking through the tent flap.

Jasper is waiting for her outside, along with the two officers. Juniper only has time to wave goodbye to Rhodie and Willow as the rabbits make a quick about face and begin marching down the footpath. Jasper escorts Juniper, and she follows the officers through tunnels of low-hanging blackberry vines to a part of the Bramble she has never explored. Just when the shafts of sunlight filtering through the leaves begin to turn blue and purple with nightfall and the pads on the bottom of Juniper's feet begin to ache, they come to a wide clearing dotted with several large tents. Beyond them, she can see the shadowy outlines of a rudimentary archery range and obstacle course.

"This will be your barracks, miss," the taller rabbit announces when they come to a stop in front of the first tent.

"I've got it from here, thank you," Jasper nods.

"You are dismissed."

"Yes, sir," The rabbits salute Jasper before disappearing into the darkness.

"Welcome to Camp Marshall," Jasper says. As her eyes adjust to the dimness of the large tent, lit only by rows of flickering candles, six rows of bunk beds come into focus. The space is warm and abuzz with movement as a dozen new trainees move about the space, unpacking belongings and chattering anxiously with fellow recruits.

There are several creatures Juniper has never seen before. Her heart leaps into her throat at the sight of a young bobcat playfully boxing with a rodent-like animal that appears to be covered in pine needles. Her eyes pass over a mole, a gopher, and several squirrels that look to be about Juniper's age. Her stomach flips and a rush of heat fills her chest when her eyes settle on a familiar gray face. Ash.

"What's *he* doing here?"

She hasn't seen her foster brother since he'd betrayed their family, leading the weasels directly to Foster Hollow. In Juniper's mind, he is the reason Sorrel's home was ripped to pieces.

"Hey, keep your voice down," Jasper warns. "We're desperate for soldiers, June."

"Clearly," Juniper grits her teeth, and Jasper steers her to a corner of the tent away from the other recruits.

"I believe he's truly sorry for what he's done. He's been counseled and is on probation. You'll learn the Values of the Archers soon enough. One of them is mercy."

"How can we trust him?" Juniper asks, anger boiling in her stomach.

"We'll be watching him. Closely."

Juniper jerks her arm away from her brother and tosses her knapsack onto the bottom mattress of what appears to be an unclaimed bunk. She shrieks in surprise when a black creature pops up from the bed frame shadows. For a split second, she thinks she's looking at an upside-down field mouse with wings.

"Oh! Sorry I scared you. I'm Dahlia," the furry flier replies, extending a small hand in welcome.

Juniper blinks, and she remembers seeing drawings of animals like this in one of Sorrel's books about nocturnal creatures. She has never had an opportunity to see a bat in the flesh before, and it takes her a moment to find her voice.

"Juniper." She returns the handshake. "Nice to meet you, Dahlia."

"Likewise." Dahlia's tiny white teeth flash with a smile. "You can take the top bunk."

"Thanks." Juniper picks up her knapsack and tosses it onto the mattress above them.

"Lights out in ten minutes, cadets!" a raccoon calls, squeezing past them.

"I guess this is it," Jasper says. "I'll let you get acquainted with your new friends." He tousles the fur between her ears before turning to leave. Juniper grabs his paw.

"Wait. What if I can't do this, Jasper? What if I'm not good enough to be an Archer?"

"You're a Spark, sis. You'll be fine."

At the sound of her family name, Juniper reaches up to touch the smooth piece of amber hanging at the base of her neck.

Spark. Her heart swells with pride and a sense of belonging. *I'm a Spark.*

"Get some sleep. You'll need it," her brother says, disappearing through the tent flap.

What feels like a few moments later, Juniper is tossing and turning beneath scratchy covers on the top bunk. She peers over the edge of the bed to see a faint outline of Dahlia hanging upside down and resting peacefully, her feet clinging to the wooden mattress frame. Somewhere in the dark, Ash is also settling into sleep. To Juniper's knowledge, he is not yet aware of her presence.

A pang of sadness grips her chest when she remembers how close she and her foster brother had been until recent months. He had been a gentle, kind squirrel that would never have done anything to hurt her—or so she'd thought. That was before he practically welcomed the weasels into their foster home. *How could he have done such a thing?*

Juniper realizes her bottom lip is trembling with emotion. She bites it and rolls over, pulling the pillow over her head to quiet the sobs that have gotten stuck in her throat. She fears they will break free any moment now.

Yesterday evening, Juniper had been reading with Sorrel in the quiet of her tent, unsure of her future but also relatively unworried about what the next day might hold. Tonight, she is on an exhilarating new path she cannot turn back from. Like her own paws in the dark in front of her, she can't see the next step she must take on this new adventure.

In spite of the fear and anxiety threatening to unravel her, words from the pages of the Book drift into her mind, bringing her inexplicable comfort and lulling her to sleep while tears dampen her sheets. *"The Light will once again overtake the darkness; until then, we must trust in faith to guide us, relying not on what we can see..."*

EIGHT
CAMP MARSHALL

It is still nighttime when Juniper wakes with a start, certain the world has come crashing down upon her. In the shapeless dark, loud banging seems to be coming from every direction. It takes her a moment to remember where she is—and realize the wild racket that stirred her awake is actually a squad of soldiers running through the barracks, banging wooden pots and pans to rouse the new recruits.

"Get up, cadets!" She hears unfamiliar voices call from below. "Outside in two minutes! Hustle!"

The announcement is followed by groans and the scurry of hurried paws. Juniper wipes the sleep from her eyes and bounds down the ladder, taking two steps at a time. She checks the bed frame for Dahlia, but her bunkmate appears to have already headed outdoors.

Juniper falls into a stumbling line of cadets, between the bobcat and spiky, rodent-like animal she saw yesterday, and follows them out into the chilly early morning air. A few moments later she is standing in the middle of the clearing just outside the barracks.

Scanning the line-up, Juniper spots Dahlia in the front row. Right-side up, the bat looks small and crumpled, like a black, wet blanket. As if she can feel Juniper's eyes on her back, Dahlia turns toward her and gives her a wide grin. Juniper can't help but return the smile. There's something unusual and endearing about her.

When the last of the soldiers-in-training fall in, the raccoon from the night before instructs them to stand shoulder-to-shoulder with paws (or wings, depending on the anatomy) pressed firmly to their sides before disappearing again, leaving them to stand in the empty field for what feels like eons.

"What're we waiting for?" The bobcat whispers out of the corner of her mouth. Juniper shrugs uneasily, afraid to move a muscle for fear of being reprimanded. The ground glitters with dew reflecting the moonlight, and curling wisps of fog give the clearing an eerie appearance. Juniper wraps her tail around her shoulders for warmth, wishing she were back in her bunk. Just when her eyelids begin to slide shut, the raccoon reappears, stepping out of the fog and into a bright shaft of moonlight to call the cadets to attention.

"Troops! You're at Camp Marshall. I'm Sergeant Pine, one of your leaders. You're about to meet the man in charge here, Colonel Thistle. You will give him the utmost respect. Stand straight. Eyes forward. I do not want to hear you breathe."

Sergeant Pine steps to the side, and a striking red bird emerges from the shadows. From the tip of his tail to the feathered crest of his head, all the way down to the sharp bend of his scaly knees, Colonel Thistle is all points and edges. His brilliant crimson feathers are dotted with just enough gray to give him a rough yet mature, dignified appearance. Sergeant Pine offers him a respectful salute before joining three other soldiers—a swallow, a hare, and a fox squirrel—standing on the sidelines.

For a moment, the cardinal paces slowly back and forth in front of the cadets. He pulls a pine needle from the feathers under his left wing and begins to pick his beak with it as if oblivious to the dozen recruits standing at attention before him.

Finally, he breaks the silence with his low, dignified voice. "Cadets. You are all here for a purpose. We believe the predators are getting bolder... or maybe reckless out of desperation. In recent months, we've had more and more run-ins with daytime prowlers. We have reason to believe a great war is on the horizon, and we all have an important part to play in it—from the most experienced soldiers to the newest recruits like you."

A shiver runs down Juniper's tail, and she

exchanges anxious glances with the pine-needle creature standing next to her. She can't help but notice the stark contrast between the colonel's calm demeanor and the sergeants' gruff attitudes.

"While the predators fight as individuals for the good of themselves, we work together as one for the good of all of Mirren," Colonel Thistle continues. "In the coming weeks, you will learn what it takes to live the Values and carry out the duties given to the Archers."

Colonel Thistle begins to walk between the rows of recruits, appearing to size each one up when he passes.

"Stand up straighter, cadet," he comments on Dahlia's slouching appearance. She immediately cranes her neck, attempting to hold her head up higher. "Yes, sir!" The small bat squeaks.

Colonel Thistle stops in front of the curious, needled creature next to Juniper. "What's your name, hedgehog?" He asks.

Hedgehog. Once again, Juniper recalls the animal from one of Sorrel's books.

"Seed, sir."

"Do you have a family name, Seed?"

"No, sir—just Seed."

"Cadet Seed it is then. An Archer always keeps himself well-groomed. Please have one of your fellow recruits help you remove the foliage you have stuck in your, uh, spines there." Colonel Thistle gestures behind Seed, where there are indeed several leaves stuck to his prickly backside.

Seed looks frantic for a moment, turning in a circle to try to reach the unwelcome adornments. Juniper and the bobcat come to his rescue and quickly rid the hedgehog of the offense before stepping back to their places in line. Out of the corner of her eye, Juniper can see traces of gratitude and relief on Seed's face.

Colonel Thistle continues on, narrowing his eyes when he comes to a stop in front of Juniper. For a moment, a look of recognition crosses his face.

"Jewelry and personal belongings are not allowed here, Cadet..." Colonel Thistle says, leaving his sentence hanging, clearly expecting a prompt reply.

Juniper quickly finds her voice. "Spark. Cadet Spark."

Colonel Thistle nods. "Please remove your dagger and necklace, Cadet Spark. We will take care of them for you while you are in training." Juniper hesitates, covering her family stone with her paw. "You will get them back, I assure you," Colonel Thistle says kindly yet firmly. A lump takes the place of the gem at the base of her throat when she removes it and reluctantly hands her meaningful family heirlooms to the cardinal.

"Sergeant Moss, take these back to headquarters for safekeeping," he says, passing the heirlooms to the swallow at his side.

"Yes, sir." Sergeant Moss accepts the items and flits away.

Juniper concentrates on fighting tears and maintaining her composure while Colonel Thistle completes his inspection. She didn't realize how comforting the weight of the amber stones on her neck and hip had been until they are no longer there.

After several more abrupt interactions, the colonel finally returns to his spot in front of the clearing. "Recruits, it's time to meet your squad leaders," he announces, motioning for the sergeants to join him. "You will now be divided into four groups based on the skills and abilities inherent to your species: climbers, fliers, burrowers, and rangers. Once you have been organized, you will be dismissed to begin your first day's exercises. Blessings to you all."

Juniper is called forward to join the climber crew, and two squirrels join her, including Ash. When Juniper's foster brother meets her eyes for the first time since they arrived, he looks as though he has been punched in the stomach. Juniper turns away, pretending to be unfazed by his presence.

The sorting continues with the fliers, who consist of Dahlia, the bat, along with Holly, a wren, and Maple, a woodpecker. Seed falls into line behind a gopher named Lavender, and a mole, Dandelion, rounding out the burrowers.

While the first three groups are based on obvious characteristics, rangers are typically four-legged, carnivorous creatures like Sitka who have not chosen the predatory lifestyle; the bobcat is grouped with a pair of pine martens, Oak and Huckleberry, that remind Juniper too much of the weasels that ransacked Foster Hollow. She shivers as she watches Sergeant Pine, a raccoon and ranger, himself, lead the first group away from the clearing.

The swallow and hare, Sergeants Moss and Clover, lead their respective groups away as well. Finally, the climbers are introduced to their squad leader: Sergeant Pollen, a fox squirrel.

"Let's get a move on, cadets!" Sergeant Pollen rubs his paws together. "There's no room for lolly-gaggers on my squad."

"Yes, sir!" Juniper's voice blends in with the others'.

Sergeant Pollen turns swiftly, leading the climbers away from the clearing and into the shadows surrounding them.

"HUP, two, three, four..."

"Hey, can we talk?" Ash whispers over Sergeant Pollen's cadence call. He is jogging closely behind

Juniper, following Sergeant Pollen on the track around the obstacle course. They have been learning to march and run together as a unit, matching stride for stride and rhythm for rhythm, for the last hour-and-a-half. The sun is rising, and the air has warmed to a comfortable temperature. Still, the sound of Ash's voice makes Juniper's blood run cold.

"I have nothing to say to you," Juniper whispers, slightly lifting her chin in annoyance.

"HUP, two—too slow, cadets! Hustle!"

"Then, can you listen?"

"HUP, two, three—am I talking to myself? I need you to *move!*"

"You're going to get us in trouble," she shoots back.

Juniper concentrates on the rhythm of her feet when Sergeant Pollen suddenly veers off the track and leads them into a tunnel of blackberry vines.

"HUP, two, three, four... "

A root appears in their path, and Juniper sees it just in time, leaping over it before falling back into the steady jogging rhythm. Ash, on the other hand, is too preoccupied with his quest to get Juniper's attention. He stumbles over the obstruction and crashes into her. Juniper loses her balance and rolls over the squirrel in front of her.

Before she realizes what has happened, she is on the ground with the rest of the squad, including a dazed and fuming Sergeant Pollen. Just one look at his furrowed eyebrows tells Juniper this isn't going to be good.

"One-hundred push ups!" Sergeant Pollen calls through gritted teeth, spit flying. "I don't care how you make it happen between the two of you—I just want to see sweat and hear you counting to one-hundred!" Pollen turns to address the others. "The rest of you, sprint to the archery range and back until they've given me what they owe. The longer it takes, the longer your fellow soldiers suffer, cadets."

Juniper glares at Ash, who averts his eyes and lowers himself into position to begin the exercise.

Despite Juniper's grievance over being teamed up with Ash, the first day of training—just like the ones that follow—goes by in a blur. After marching and breakfast in the mess hall, the morning is filled with a strenuous obstacle course and strengthening exercises, then lunch and countless laps around the archery range in the afternoon. Juniper's head hangs heavy over her feet when Sergeant Pollen finally releases the climbers for dinner.

Juniper frowns as she watches the sweaty soldier scoop ladles of lumpy pudding onto her plate next to a hard acorn biscuit, similar to the lunch and breakfast she'd devoured earlier.

"Thank you," she smiles at the cook anyway, and

turns to find a table.

The mess hall is unusually quiet. Drooping eyelids and hunched postures make it evident that the new recruits have been pushed to their limit.

Juniper puts her tray down at the end of an unoccupied picnic table and settles in to eat. Her spoon feels like it weighs a hundred pounds. She can barely lift it to her mouth. Just when she manages to successfully swallow her first spoonful of pudding, another tray plunks onto the table next to hers.

"Mind if I sit here?" the bobcat asks.

Juniper shakes her head. "Not at all. Help yourself."

"I'm Daphne," she says, settling onto the bench.

"Juniper. Nice to meet you."

"Likewise. It's been a long day, right?"

All Juniper can do is nod slightly.

"Hey, Seed! Spike! Over here!" Daphne waves over the hedgehog and fox squirrel, who make their way over to the table to join them. Dahlia follows suit, and a few moments later, Ash slides in next to her.

Of all the tables he could've picked... Juniper rolls her eyes.

"So, where are you all from?" Daphne asks, snapping her biscuit in half with one large paw. "They found me in the forest when I was just a cub. Same with Seed, right, buddy? We've been at Bramble Academy ever since, waiting for this our whole lives, pretty much."

The hedgehog nods enthusiastically.

"Where are you from, Dahlia?" Daphne asks over a mouthful of biscuit. "You're the first bat I've ever met."

The sentiment trickles around the table, and Dahlia seems pleased with the attention. "I'm from the last family of bats on this side of The Waste," she says in a small voice. "It's tradition that we serve when we're old enough. I'm the eldest of three sisters—the first bat to come to Logan Bramble since my papa served in the Unraveling." She turns her attention to the squirrel sitting next to her. "What about you?"

"I'm Spikerush," he says, looking down at his paws. "But you can call me Spike."

"Where do you come from, Spike?" Daphne asks.

"My family..." Spike begins. He pauses for a moment, swallowing hard. "My whole family was taken by predators last summer. I came here looking for help. I didn't know where else to go."

The ache of compassion fills Juniper's chest. "I'm so sorry, Spike," she says quietly, and the others nod with sympathy. She searches her heart for appropriate words of comfort to share but finds none.

Daphne does her best to turn the attention away from Spike when the stretch of silence lingers a little too long. "How about you, Juniper? Ash?"

"I—" Juniper begins, but Ash cuts her off.

"Juniper and I grew up in a place called Foster Hollow," he says.

Before she can reign it in, a flash of anger causes bitter words to spew from her mouth. "Yes. And then Ash destroyed it." Juniper stands abruptly. "Excuse me," she says, trying to avoid the surprised eyes and confused expressions she feels on her back while she strides across the mess hall and out into the evening air.

Laying in her bunk at night, Juniper pictures Dahlia dangling upside-down from the bed frame beneath her. She hears the other soldiers' muffled snores. Even though she is surrounded by living, breathing creatures, Juniper can't shake the suffocating feeling she is all alone.

Her cheeks flush with heat when she remembers how she behaved at dinner this evening. She feels embarrassed and ashamed—but also angry and justified somehow. Hot tears sting her eyes, and she rolls over to keep them from dampening her pillow.

Juniper has only been here for one full day, and she is already overwhelmed with loneliness for Sorrel and the kids. She doesn't have a home—not really, anyway—but she is homesick for the feelings of comfort, safety, and kinship her foster family and friends provide. She wishes she could confide her feelings in Rhodie and Willow. They would understand. Even Sitka's sarcasm would be a welcome distraction from the heartache creeping into her bunk. She squeezes her eyes shut and lets the tears roll down her cheeks, too tired to fight them.

Sleep now, she hears Sorrel's voice like an echo in her heart. *Rest, for tomorrow is a new day.* Juniper closes her eyes. Soon, she is dreaming of a swooping red-tailed hawk, slashing talons, and falling into bottomless darkness.

NINE
CAPTAIN SPARK

Heavy, purple clouds darken the canopy of blackberry vines above the archery range. The smell of wet soil makes Juniper shiver in spite of the unseasonably warm, humid morning air. She isn't looking forward to spending the day any damper than usual. Sweat is already bad enough.

Juniper breathes a sigh of relief when she spots Jasper's confident form among the sergeants standing in front of the target line. It's been two weeks since she last saw her brother—the same day she arrived at Camp Marshall. Juniper had begun to worry he'd been called away on a more important mission. Sure, he'd agreed to oversee her training, but he certainly had more meaningful things to do all day than shout at a bunch of new recruits to give him "one more" push up or lap around the range, which is what Juniper expected they'd be doing now; these activities have been the highlight of training up to this point.

The hours making up the last fourteen days have smeared together in an exhausting blur of dirt, noise, and muscle strain. Juniper has been pushed to her physical limit before collapsing into her bunk each night, where she continues to run from sharp claws and shadowy birds of prey in fitful dreams.

Her brother's fiery red fur appears brighter than usual in the threatening storm's gray gloom; it brings her a sense of comfort she hasn't felt since he'd tousled the hair between her ears and calmed her with the words, "You're a Spark, sis. You'll be fine." She holds his reminder close to her heart—where the amber stone should be—in the many moments she is too tired to keep going.

Jasper pretends not to notice her at first, his eyes skimming over hers without a hint of recognition. He struts across the training ground, nodding to soldiers as he passes, before eventually coming to a stop at Juniper's left, his back to her.

"How's it going?" He whispers out of the corner of his mouth. "You look like you haven't slept in days."

Juniper rolls her eyes. "I'm fine," she whispers. "I can handle it. The worst thing that's happened so far has been Colonel Thistle taking the dagger and my necklace."

"Yeah, don't worry about that," Jasper assures her. "You'll get them back. He's one of the good guys. Dad's friend."

Did I hear that right? Colonel Thistle, our father's friend? She tries to picture an older version of

Jasper with an edge like the cardinal, but her thoughts scatter when Sergeant Pollen calls the cadets to attention.

"I'm sure you were all looking forward to another day of strenuous exercise, recruits, but we're moving on to the next phase of your training. Captain Jasper Spark will be stepping in to teach you the foundations of archery. You will listen, give him your full attention, and be respectful. Do not disappoint me."

The soldiers stomp their feet in unison to express their excitement. Juniper is always one of the last to join in. The group gesture they'd been conditioned to perform feels forced and awkward.

"Your first few weeks were about conditioning," Jasper begins without further pleasantries. "Now, you're ready to learn the ways of the Archer." He pauses, giving the young soldiers another opportunity to stamp with appreciation.

"Today, we'll begin with archery basics. I need a volunteer to join me on the range."

Ash is the first to step forward, which annoys Juniper but doesn't surprise her. He has been going out of his way to present himself in the best possible light.

"What's your name, cadet?" Jasper asks, feigning ignorance.

"Cadet Ash, sir."

"Very well, Cadet Ash. Together, we're going to demonstrate how to help an arrow find its target." He lifts a slender bow from a wooden rack where there are more than a dozen curved branches hanging, shiny and ready for use. Ash accepts the weapon from Jasper while the captain chooses another for himself.

"Your bow should feel light, almost weightless. How's yours, cadet?"

Ash nods in approval. "Just right, sir."

"Excellent. When you're ready to aim, stand crosswise to your target."

Jasper beckons Ash to follow him when he takes several steps closer to the wooden slab set up a few yards ahead of them. He plants his feet and angles himself so he is perpendicular to the red mark, gesturing for Ash to follow suit.

"The two most important things to remember are consistency and comfort," Jaspers calls over his shoulder, loud enough for all the cadets to hear.

"You will rest the string on the pad of your paw or the tip of your wing. As you draw back and position your arrow, you should feel more tension in your back than your shoulders."

Jasper pauses while Ash fiddles with the bow string until he finds a relaxed position, pulling both the string and arrow back to match the captain's stance.

"Good. Now, bring the arrow to your eye and

hold it steady at an easy anchor point, where it feels like a natural resting place." Jaspers pauses for a moment, waiting for Ash to catch up. "Everything—your arm, your elbow, and the arrow shaft—should now be in a straight line."

"To aim true, the tip of your arrow should be pointing slightly left," he continues. "As you draw back, it will move to the right, towards the center of the target."

Ash raises his eyebrows to ask for feedback on his stance, and Jasper dips his chin in validation.

"When you're ready to shoot, bring your paw or wing-tip to your shoulder. Don't waste your concentration on aiming at this point. You've done that part already, and your mind will take over for you. Trust it. Focus on the release, and let the string slip from your grasp."

Juniper is impressed by her brother's eloquent lesson. He can be serious when he wants to be. She watches Ash's arrow follow Jasper's in an elegant arch, striking the target just to the right of the captain's bullseye hit. She has to admit, he's a good teacher.

"Excellent," Jasper grins. "That's how it's done. You're a natural, Cadet Ash."

A pang of jealousy shoots through Juniper when the captain gives Ash a congratulatory slap on the back.

"Now, the rest of you... move forward while we issue your bows one at a time. We're going to begin close to the target and step back as we get more and more comfortable with the distance."

The captains begin handing out equipment to the remaining eleven recruits. Captain Pollen selects a medium-sized branch for Juniper. It's sleek, but also cumbersome somehow. The carved wood doesn't fit in the curve of her paw the way her slingshot does.

Juniper casts an anxious glance up to the sky. The violet clouds still lurk above them, but the storm appears to be holding off for now. She takes a few steps forward and positions herself in front of a target the way Jasper showed them. She raises her bow and pulls the empty string back and forth, testing its strength and flexibility. Out of the corner of her eye, she watches Jasper as he makes his way down the line, offering words of advice and encouragement to his students.

"Raise your shoulder, cadet," he says as he passes Dahlia. "Get your elbow down. That's better."

Jasper pauses in front of Juniper. Feeling his eyes on her, she fumbles with the arrow when she fits it into place. "Careful," Jasper warns. "Take your time, cadet."

Juniper pulls the string taught and winces as a twinge of pain runs through her shoulder. The wound the owl gave her the night she met Jasper has healed nicely, but the scar is still tender. Juniper waits for the stinging to subside before she closes one eye, takes a deep breath, and releases the arrow. The thunk it makes when it hits the target is satisfying. It's a solid shot, but her shoulder is tight, which is exactly what Jasper had said to avoid.

"Good shot," he compliments her anyway. *Had he noticed the grimace?*

"It doesn't feel natural," Juniper says with a scowl.

"It doesn't feel natural *yet*," Jasper corrects her. "Keep practicing, Cadet Spark."

"I prefer my slingshot," Juniper says just loud enough for her brother to hear.

As usual, Ash is already sitting next to Daphne, Seed, and Spike when Juniper enters the mess hall for lunch. She he averts her gaze and slides into an empty bench on the other side of the tent.

"Can I sit with you?" A small voice asks. She looks up to see Dahlia.

Juniper shrugs and nods. The two eat quietly for a moment. The only audible noise above the excited din of lunchroom chatter are the sounds of their wooden spoons scraping the bottoms of their bowls. Dahlia is first to break the silence.

"I couldn't help but notice you and Captain Spark share the same family name, and you look alike.

Are you related?"

Juniper nods sheepishly. "He's my brother."

Dahlia chews on this bit of information along with the bits of nuts in her pudding.

"What about Ash? I heard he's your brother, too, but he doesn't look like you at all. Is he?"

Juniper's stomach flips at the unexpected course the conversation has taken. She is quiet for a moment, considering how to answer the question.

"No... and yes," she says. "It's complicated."

"Can I ask what you meant when you said that stuff about him destroying your home? Foster Hollow? Is that true?"

Juniper swallows a mouthful of pecan pudding and looks up at Dahlia's large, innocent black eyes. *Yes*, she wants to say. *He's the reason it's in shambles.*

"No, not really," she sighs, choosing the truth instead. "He was mixed up in a series of events that led up to it... but, it wasn't his fault."

Dahlia is sensitive to Juniper's vague response, and she decides not to press further. After another moment of awkward silence, Juniper gets up the nerve to ask her own bold question.

"You said it's tradition in your family to serve as an archer when you come of age. What was it like growing up, knowing this was your path from the beginning?"

Dahlia swallows the last bite of mush. "It was

exciting, I guess. And, comforting in a way, because I didn't have to think too much about the future. But, also... lots of pressure. I've heard stories that have been passed down for generations—some adventurous and exciting. Some terrifying."

Dahlia bites her bottom lip, anxiety showing on her tiny face. "I don't want to let my family down."

"Yeah, I can relate to that feeling," Juniper frowns.

Their conversation ends abruptly when Sergeant Pine calls the troops to attention, signaling the end of lunchtime.

"Nice talking to you," Dahlia whispers, grinning.

"Likewise," Juniper smiles back, and she means it. For the first time since she arrived at Camp Marshall, Juniper feels like she has made a friend.

Juniper stands to put her tray away and follow Dahlia to the exit. She isn't sure, but she thinks she can feel Ash's eyes on her back as she finds her place in the line of soldiers already forming behind the sergeant.

TEN
ARCHER VALUES

A crack of thunder announces the storm's arrival just as Sergeant Pine ushers the last of the recruits into the large tent next to the mess hall. Juniper is surprised to discover the shelter is filled with rows of individual desks, bookshelves, and writing materials. An ache in her chest reminds her how much she misses Sorrel.

Juniper settles into a seat behind Dahlia, welcoming the change of pace. Flickering candles light the dim space, giving it a cozy, sleepy atmosphere. Rain patters softly on the tent canvas above her, and her head and eyelids suddenly feel heavy. *If only I can keep from nodding off...*

"All right, cadets!"

The dozen recruits jolt upright in unison at the loud smack of a stick striking the desk at the front of the tent. Colonel Thistle materializes from the shadows, his small black eyes capturing his students' full attention.

"Battlefield success depends on more than

physical swiftness and skill," he begins as if in the middle of a lecture.

"It depends on the mind and heart of the Archer, as well—the willingness to use your own skill sets and strengths to work as individual parts in one body of soldiers; the bravery of valuing others as you value yourself—putting others before yourself, if you so dare."

A gust of wind bursts through the tent flap, ruffling fur and feathers, and snuffing out every candle its path. "Now, that's appropriate," Colonel Thistle chuckles uncharacteristically, seemingly amused by the sudden blackout. He clears his throat and continues speaking while sergeants rush around the tent, relighting smoking wicks.

"Darkness makes it so we can't see each other. We can only focus on ourselves and our own desires and emotions. It is all consuming. This is how Mirren fell into the hands of the predators—pride, greed, and thirst for power."

"From here on out, you will begin your day with physical fitness and archery foundations, and you will end it here in the classroom, where we will discuss the history, duty, and Values of the Archers."

"This afternoon, we will take a birds-eye view—" The cardinal pauses, glaring, when a giggle bursts forth from the last row of students, but the laughter is quickly dampened. He moves on. "We'll take a birds-eye view of Mirren's history, how we got where we are today, and the hopes we hold for the future."

Juniper gasps when a heavy book lands on her desk with a loud thump. She is so captivated by Colonel Thistle's speech, she hadn't noticed the sergeants passing out copies of the Book of Mirren to each cadet.

"The Ever Tree and the River Lasting are illustrated on the cover of the volume in front of you. This is the Book of Mirren. Many of you may have your own copy. For others, this is the first time you will be hearing of it, not to mention reading its passages. Together, we'll be examining portions of it together, as it was written for us all as a history, reminder, and love letter."

Juniper wrinkles her nose. *Love* letter? The passages feel more like a warning than a note of adoration.

Colonel Thistle turns and unfurls a weathered map on the canvas wall behind him. Isle of Mirren is penned in dramatic cursive letters above the craggy outline of an island. Juniper recognizes the thick cluster of trees to the south, notating the Dark Forest; somewhere within those groves lies Logan Bramble, Camp Marshall, and what's left of Foster Hollow. The Waste and the vast mountain range where Jacob's Lair lies fills the space in the center and to the northwest portions of the map, respectively. The rocky land and large body of water to the northeast, however, are entirely unfamiliar to Juniper.

"It is said the Maker of Mirren, our own Creator, dwells within the elements and beyond. The Ever Tree, which is pictured on the front of your book, is the life source of our island; the River Lasting burst forth from an underground spring beneath the Tree's roots, bringing water and vitality to all the land."

"For a long time, an Alliance representing every species of Mirren maintained law, order, peace and justice for the good of all—until animals turned from wisdom." The fur on the back of Juniper's neck raises when she remembers these are the very words her brother had spoken around the campfire the night he'd tumbled into her life.

"They began to live by their instincts and go after what was rightfully theirs," he'd said. *"Predators, for example, were not satisfied with their share. They began to hurt and take more and more."* She'd since read this passage in the Book of Mirren over and over again. When Juniper asked how Jasper could possibly believe the old stories of Mirren are true, he replied with one puzzling word: *"Faith."*

Colonel Thistle continues. "The predators, who were first created to protect the Ever Tree and uphold balance in all of Mirren, misunderstood the Tree's part in it all," he says. "They saw its great power and wanted to harness it for themselves."

"A group of predators and prey, alike, banded together. They betrayed the First Alliance and blocked the River at its three tributaries—one near Jacob's Lair, where the River once emptied into Cypress Bay; another at the base of the mountains, which is now called The Waste; the last at the mouth of Richie Gorge." Colonel Thistle turns to the map and points his stick at the locations he is referencing. "This is known as the Unraveling—the undoing of our way of life."

Jasper had said their grandfather, Alder, had been one of the traitors that had a hand in redirecting the River. Juniper swallows a knot in her throat.

"Water rose, Mirren flooded, and..." The colonel pauses while he circles an area north of Richie Gorge that now depicts a lake. "The Ever Tree was lost, along with countless homes and families." Sorrel's face appears in Juniper's mind. She was one of the victims who'd lost everything.

"Before it succumbed to the rising waters, however, the great Tree bestowed seven gifts upon its protectors. These treasures are said to offer hope for the restoration of Mirren."

There is a weighty silence. Thunder rumbles and rain pounds on the cloth overhead.

"What *are* the gifts? Where are they now?" A soldier calls out without permission. Juniper turns to see who is brazen enough to interrupt the colonel.

Daphne. Sergeant Pine motions to silence the bobcat, but Colonel Thistle raises a wing to stop him.

"We're not certain," he answers. "Believed to have powerful properties, they've been hunted by the predators for years. There are theories and prophecies, of course, but many of them conflict with one another. The only truths we can count on are written in the Book of Mirren: we are all made by the Creator, precious and loved; we are all broken creatures in a land lost to the Unraveling, which was our own undoing, I might add; and, there will come a day when our Maker will set things right, as they were intended."

"When that day comes, we will have to defeat our greatest adversaries—the predators, of course, and also ourselves. The greatest mission of the Archers is to live out our Values and rebuild the Alliance so we are ready when the day of fighting comes."

"Why do we have to wait? Why can't we attack first?" Daphne interrupts again. "Why doesn't the Creator help us now?"

"All excellent questions." Juniper is surprised to find Colonel Thistle more patient than she would have guessed. "As for why we can't attack first—that is not the way of the Archer. We believe in love, mercy, justice. Self-discipline, service, and selflessness. Firing the first shot, fully knowing the sacrifice and pain of war, goes against everything we believe in. The answers to your other queries will be revealed in time, soldier." Colonel Thistle pauses to clear his throat. "Now, speaking of self-discipline, service, and selflessness—that's all for today," he says with finality. "You've heard enough of my voice. Your homework tonight is to read the first and second chapters of the Book."

When Colonel Thistle exits as quietly as he arrived, it feels like a trance is broken inside the tent. Juniper's head is spinning. She glances at her fellow soldiers, who, like her, are now fidgeting uncomfortably in their seats, anticipating whatever comes next.

Could they all believe the cardinal's wild claims? An unseen Maker lives within the island's elements? A tree is the life source of Mirren? Juniper doesn't find it hard to believe her ancestors played a part in the destruction, but trusting in an invisible force to make things right doesn't seem logical or wise. Juniper's forehead wrinkles in confusion. Words she'd read in the Book of Mirren the last time she studied with Sorrel flit across her mind, unprompted.

"The Light will once again overtake the darkness; until then, we must trust in faith to guide us, relying not on what we can see..."

There's that complicated word again. *What does faith really mean?*

Juniper isn't given much time to reflect before Sergeant Pollen steps into the center of the tent to draw the cadets' attention back to the classroom.

"Today marks the halfway point in your training. Your final test, a field exercise assessing your individual skill, fitness, and character, will take place in two weeks. Your performance will determine whether or not you graduate and earn the rank of lieutenant."

"Before you're dismissed, you will be given a slip of paper indicating the soldier with whom you have been randomly paired to train with from here on out."

At this announcement, Sergeants Pine, Moss, and Clover begin moving about the tent to pass out assignments. Juniper carefully unfolds the slip of paper she is handed, somehow already knowing the name scribbled upon it: *Ash*.

ELEVEN
MERCY

Juniper's pine cone porridge sits heavy in her stomach. She would rather spend the day cleaning out Flint the Black's underground lair after months of hibernation than partner with Ash in training exercises today. Her stomach turns when she sees the young squirrel already speaking with Captain Spark while other cadets find their places on the archery range.

Jasper has his hand on Ash's shoulder and looks to be giving him a pep talk. Ash is probably trying to worm his way out of having to spend the day in misery, which is what Juniper was also hoping to accomplish. The defeated look on Ash's face tells her it's a lost cause.

"Good mornin', Cadet Spark." Jasper grins when he locks eyes with his sister, clearly amused by the sour expression on her face. "Nice to see you so bright-eyed and bushy-tailed."

Juniper ignores him. She has the feeling her brother had something to do with her partner assignment.

"Hey," Ash approaches cautiously, looking at the ground.

"Hey," Juniper responds flatly, falling in line next to him. Fortunately, the vigorous training schedule doesn't leave much room for small talk. Before another awkward moment passes, Jasper steps away from the two to call the cadets to attention.

"Good morning, troops. If you haven't already noticed, there are only six targets on the range today. From here on out, the cadet next to you will be your spotter. While one has a turn at the bow, the other will serve the shooter by presenting and retrieving arrows as needed."

The archery range is bright and cheerful this morning despite Juniper's gloomy mood. Yesterday's storm had washed away layers of dust and dirt that had settled on Camp Marshall since the last time it rained, and the air feels clean and crisp.

"Now, take a moment to introduce yourselves, if you haven't already, and decide who will be collecting your equipment."

Juniper flips her tail nervously when the cadets around her begin turning to one another to offer hasty greetings. "Let's get this over with, shall we?" She grumbles. "I'll shoot first."

Ash nods in agreement. "I'll collect the arrows."

The morning is less painful than Juniper

expects. Ash is a quiet, respectful partner, and they each fulfill their duties without unnecessary commentary. It's obvious Juniper's practice with her slingshot has given her an advantage on the archery range; however, she is frustrated to see more of Ash's arrows hit the center of the target than hers.

After lunch, the cadets march back to the classroom with bellies full of pine bark biscuits and wild onion soup. Juniper scans the dimly lit space and spots Dahlia seated next to Daphne. The meek bat and bold bobcat are an awkward pair. Next to them, Spike and Seed seem to be the only two taking part in comfortable conversation. Juniper casts a glance at Ash from the corner of her eye and notices he is jiggling his leg nervously under his desk.

Sergeant Pine pulls Juniper's attention to the front of the classroom. "Cadets, turn to page eighteen in the Book of Mirren, where you'll find the Values of the Archers. Today, you and your partner will be assigned one of the six foundational themes to study together. When one hour is up, you will choose a presenter, who will share what you have learned with the class."

Of the six Values, Juniper knows exactly which one she *doesn't* want to research with Ash—the one Jasper had said would help her understand why he'd been allowed to participate in training at all.

"*I believe he's truly sorry for what he's done. He's*

been counseled and is on probation. You'll learn the Values of the Archers soon enough," he'd said. *"One of them is mercy."*

Juniper prays silently as the sergeants hand out strips of paper once again. *Please don't be that one, please don't be that one, please don't be...*

She holds her breath as she watches Ash accept the slip from Sergeant Pollen and unfold it. "Ours is... mercy," he reads aloud.

Juniper groans audibly. *Jasper. I'll get him back for this.*

⁓∞⁓

Juniper and Ash read quietly side by side. When the hour is up, Juniper passes Ash a page of notes she has prepared for both of them. "Here," she says.

"Thanks." Ash accepts the paper from her outstretched paw. "I'll be the presenter."

Juniper doesn't argue.

When Sergeant Moss asks for a pair to present voluntarily, Daphne is the first to raise her paw. Dahlia follows her to the front of the room, looking anxious and vulnerable next to her confident partner. The bobcat is thrilled, of course, to be the center of attention. Juniper's eyes glaze over as Daphne launches into a detailed description of the Archer Value of love.

Ash's paw shoots into the air when the rumble of complimentary stomping accompanies Dahlia and

Daphne back to their desks. "We'll go next," he says.

Juniper is reluctant to leave her seat, but she stands and takes her place at the front of the classroom next to her partner.

"Our value is mercy," Ash says, swallowing hard. "The Book of Mirren says mercy is *'extending compassion and goodwill, particularly to those who have done wrong.'*"

Juniper's eyebrows furrow when she watches Ash crumple the edges of the paper with his paws. What he says next is definitely not written in her notes.

"Particularly someone like me. I did something terrible. A group of weasels told me they would help me find my family if I gave them the hidden location of my foster home." Ash shifts uncomfortably and clears his throat. "I was so desperate, I betrayed my foster mother, sisters, and brothers. I don't deserve to be here with you all today, but I am. To me, this is an example of Archers living out the Value of mercy. Thank you."

Juniper's mouth opens in dazed surprise. Before she can make a sound, Ash is already returning to his seat with slumped shoulders and his eyes on the ground.

※

The next two weeks go by in a similar fashion. Aside from the variation in classroom lessons, each day is a repetition of the one before. Unlike the first half of training, Juniper is more mentally than physically exhausted when she climbs into her bunk at night. Her eyes are strained from reading countless passages of the Book, her paw cramps from writing pages of notes, and her head aches from the emotional drain of spending her days paired with Ash. Juniper is proud of herself when she manages to go the entire two weeks without speaking more than a few whole sentences to her partner. The rush of pride is followed by a pang of shame. She can only guess how disappointed Sorrel would be.

When the day of the final test arrives, Juniper wakes with anxious energy, eager to get the field exercise over with. Though she is encouraged to eat as much as she can for the long day's journey ahead, she barely tastes the lumpy lichen porridge she is served at breakfast.

The first shafts of sunlight filter through the blackberry vines while the cadets stand in line to receive their bows and quivers, along with knapsacks full of necessities.

When instructed, Juniper dumps the contents of her pack onto the ground to take inventory of the items: tent materials, an extra tunic, a basic tool set, a wooden cot frame, two days' ration of dried nuts and berries, and a small canteen filled with rainwater.

Jasper's tell-tale shadow falls over Juniper just as she fits the last item back into her bag. "You ready to hit the trail, cadet?"

"At least I know it's an exercise this time." Juniper smirks at her brother. She stands and slides her knapsack over her left shoulder.

"Godspeed," he says with a wink.

Juniper gives her brother a genuine smile before turning to follow the line of cadets leading into the tunnel of vines beyond the archery range.

Juniper can't be sure, but she thinks they've passed the same red-and-white spotted toadstool a dozen times now. *Are we walking in circles?*

She has long-since lost the battle of keeping sweat out of her eyes. Rivers of salt are now streaming down her face, matting her fur in dark, orange stripes. Despite the cooler temperatures, the tunnel of blackberry vines is tight and stuffy, and the sun's warmth seems to be following them on their trek through the outer limits of Camp Marshall. *How much longer?*

Juniper is too busy studying the mushroom they seem to be passing yet again to notice when Holly, the wren, comes to an abrupt stop in front of her. She gets a mouthful of brown feathers.

"Oops, sorry," Juniper mumbles, embarrassed.

The wren giggles, shrugging it off. "We're here!"

Juniper follows Holly out of the tunnel and into a circular field where four logs have been positioned to form makeshift benches around a firepit.

"Take a seat," Sergeant Clover, the hare, motions for the soldiers to join him.

Juniper sits next to Holly, and Ash slumps onto the bark next to her. She draws her elbow back when the fur on his arm touches hers.

"We've made it to our campsite," Sergeant Clover announces. For a moment, Juniper half-expects Colonel Thistle to jump out from the surrounding foliage, but he doesn't. She is almost disappointed.

"After a brief, er, briefing, you will be setting up your tents and sorting your gear to prepare for tomorrow's exercise. Are there any questions before we get started?"

The gopher, Lavender, raises a tiny paw. "Are we safe from predators here?"

"We're never safe from predators, cadet," Sergeant Clover sternly replies.

Juniper senses apprehension in the hush that falls upon the troops.

"Any other questions?" Sergeant Clover scans the ring. When no other paw or wing is raised, he continues. "The exercise will begin at dawn tomorrow morning."

"Keep an eye out for Archers posing as enemy

predators in the woods. If you get hit with one of their blunt arrows, you'll still be allowed to participate in the exercise, but you won't be able to help your fellow cadets continue on with the mission."

"Remember your training. Remember your tools. Remember the Values. Everything else will fall into place if you focus on these points." Sergeant Clover pauses for emphasis before continuing. "Your partners are counting on you, cadets."

Juniper sneaks a sideways glance at Ash. Despite his seemingly genuine public confession in the classroom, he hasn't tried to initiate any further conversation with her since their collision on the track weeks ago. *What is he thinking?* Juniper can't help but wonder. *Will I ever be able to count on Ash again?*

TWELVE

FAILURE & FORGIVENESS

A curtain of emerald leaves comes into focus when Juniper's eyes adjust to the early morning light. There is a chill in the air that tells her the sun hasn't quite risen over the horizon, and warmth is still radiating from the smoldering embers of last night's campfire. She rolls over, the weight of much-needed rest attempting to pull her back into hazy dreams. Her eyes shoot open when she notices crumpled blankets on Ash's empty cot to her left.

Juniper jolts upright, suddenly remembering the exercise on the day's agenda. Rubbing the remnants of sleep from her eyes, she casts a panicked glance around the campsite and notices five additional cadets are missing: Daphne, Spike, and one of the weasley pine martens called Huckleberry, along with the gopher and wren, Lavender and Holly. The others are still sleeping soundly beneath thick gray blankets.

Juniper hears whistling snores coming from the cot to the right. She pokes at the lump under the covers. "Huh? What?" A mess of red and black

black feathers appears above crinkled sheets.

"They're gone!" Juniper whispers.

Maple, the woodpecker, blinks in dazed confusion. "Who?"

"Our partners!"

Juniper stifles a shriek when Oak, the second pine marten who appeared to be snoozing in his cot on the other side of the campfire, tumbles out of bed and jumps into action.

"Up and at 'em, cadets! We need to take roll to figure out who's here and who's been taken."

Dahlia, Dandelion, Seed, and Maple scurry out of bed and instinctively line up on either side of Juniper, paws and wings pressed firmly to their sides just as they'd been conditioned to do.

"Right. Just as I suspected." Oak sizes up the remaining cadets with a paw on his chin and a scowl on his face, but he doesn't elaborate. Instead, he wastes no time giving orders. "Dahlia and Maple, take to the sky and see if you can spot where they're holding them. Seed and Dandelion, scan the area to look for tracks that might tell us which direction they've headed. Juniper, ready your bow. You and I will protect the perimeter."

Juniper is about to protest but decides against it. Instead, she joins the rest of cadets when they dash off to carry out their respective duties.

A short time later, the bat and woodpecker

FAILURE AND FORGIVENESS

flutter back to the campsite. Oak, Juniper, Dandelion, and Seed gather around them, waiting to hear their report.

"Good news. We've found their location," Maple announces with apprehension in his voice. "It's about four miles to the northeast."

"The bad news is, I've already been hit." Dahlia turns to show the spot on her backside where an Archer's blunt arrow has given her a bright-red, circular stamp.

"I think it might taste like strawberry syrup." Juniper tries to hide her grin.

Dahlia raises a wing to reach the spot with her long bat tongue. "Mmm. Indeed, it does."

"Great, we already have one man down within the first hour." Oak whines with impatience. "Come on, cadets. Let's get a move on."

"Shouldn't we eat something first?" Juniper raises an eyebrow. "We'll need energy for our journey."

Oak scoffs. "We don't have time."

"We have all day," Juniper argues. Her stomach is already grumbling.

Oak leans closer and responds in hushed tones. "Have you seen these guys? We'll need every minute we have to make it four miles by nightfall."

Juniper realizes he has a point. The Archers seem to have taken the strongest cadets hostage, giving the smaller, weaker animals an opportunity to step up to the challenge. Juniper shakes off a pang of disappointment when she acknowledges she is included in this less-skilled group.

"We can pack something—"

"The weight of it will just slow us down." The pine marten is clearly irritated with her persistence. "Let's go!"

"Wait, we were told to remember our tools. You go ahead. I'm going to put a few things in a knapsack, just in case."

"Fine. Suit yourself. Come on, cadets! Follow me!" Oak is already disappearing into the foliage when the others fall into step behind him.

"Juniper, you comin'?" Dahlia pauses before ducking into the tunnel of vines, hesitant to leave without her friend.

"Go ahead. I'll catch up!"

Not even a quarter-mile into tracking, the next simulated predator attack comes sooner than Juniper expects. She ducks just in time, missing the sticky arrow that hits the tree trunk next to her with a wet smack.

"Aw, nuts and berries!" Seed protests. The hedgehog removes the shaft lodged in his spines. "They got me."

Oak swiftly pivots and sends an arrow flying

back in the direction from which the others had come. Juniper and Dahlia join in, returning fire. The ambush ceases just as quickly as it had begun.

"You all right, Seed?" Juniper asks.

"Yeah," he responds, disappointment evident in his voice.

"Let's keep moving," she encourages the troops.

A short time later, the cadets come to a clearing where a deep ravine splits the land in two. "This must be one of the River's old tributaries," Dahlia says grimly, looking down the steep ledge at what appears to be a dry riverbed below them.

"You didn't spot this from the sky?" Oak asks in an accusatory tone.

"No, it wasn't visible through the vines," Maple says, sticking up for his friend.

"It will take us a day-and-a-half just to climb down and up the other side!" Seed grumbles.

"For you, maybe, but I'm not going to wait around and see," Oak barks. "I'm tired of babysitting." With a flip of his long brown tail, he slides down the cliff and disappears in a plume of dust.

"Wait! You can't just leave us here!" Juniper calls after the pine marten.

"He already did," Dahlia squeaks, folding her arms in disgust. "What do we do now?"

Juniper swallows a lump of panic rising in her throat, scanning the surrounding foliage. A flare of hope rises in her chest when she spots a possible solution.

"Maple, if the wood is soft enough, how long would it take you to hammer through a tree trunk?"

"It depends on the size." Maple shrugs.

"How about that one?" Juniper points to a tall, rotting fir tree slumping over the ravine. Its roots have begun to trail down the cliffside in desperate search of fertile soil, dragging its crumbling trunk and branches along with it.

"I'd say... an hour. Maybe two."

Juniper glances up at the sky to locate the sun's position. It appears to be directly overhead now—midday. "Let's get to work then." Juniper drops her knapsack to the ground to retrieve the small saw she'd spotted in her toolkit. "The rest of us will do what we can to help."

The tree falls with one last battering round of Maple's chisel-like beak. He looks over at Juniper with a smile of satisfaction and relief on his face. Together, they watch the trunk land right where they want it, forming a bridge over the dangerous canyon.

"Great work, Maple," Juniper grins. The fact that Maple could have flown across the ravine in seconds, and stayed to help his friends anyway is not lost on Juniper. "Thank you."

Loose branches clatter to the bottom of the

FAILURE AND FORGIVENESS

ravine below, and the gnarled, upturned roots look menacing—like giant talons. Juniper shudders.

"Do you really think it's safe to cross?" Dandelion asks, visibly trembling.

"Hold on to my fur," Juniper responds quickly, trying not to consider the question. "We'll be fine."

Dandelion climbs onto Juniper's back. "Dahlia and Maple, you fly ahead. Seed, follow close behind me," she instructs.

Juniper's heart begins to beat wildly in her chest when she takes a few steps forward to find her balance on the fallen tree trunk. Her paws immediately sink into the soft wood.

"Okay, hold on Dandelion," Juniper braces herself, then scurries across the makeshift bridge to the other side of the ravine where Maple and Dahlia are already waiting. When Dandelion slides safely off her back and onto the ground, Juniper realizes she's been holding her breath.

"We made it! Thank you, Juniper!" Dandelion squeaks in a moment of excitement before her expression changes. "Oh, no—Seed!"

Juniper's tail goes rigid with fear when she turns to see the hedgehog still struggling to find his footing on the trunk.

"Seed! You okay?" Juniper calls.

"Uhm... I don't know. I'm not sure I can make it."

Juniper can see Seed shaking from a distance.

"Don't worry! I've got you!" She calls.

Without thinking, she dashes back across the tree. Another round of loose branches crash at the bottom of the canyon in her wake.

"You can do it, Seed. Just take one step at a time. You go first, and I'll be right behind you." Juniper does her best to sound encouraging, but she can't hide the quivering in her voice. Seed nods and steps away from the ravine, putting his full body weight on the rotting wood.

"Hey, this isn't so bad—" he begins, when the trunk begins to crumble beneath his feet.

"Go!" Juniper yells. In a panicked blur, she bounds onto the tree, wraps her arms around the hedgehog and rolls to the other side of the canyon. She doesn't feel the sting of his spines pressing into her fur until she is laying on the forest floor on the other side, working to catch her breath.

"Yowch! Those things are dangerous!" Juniper laughs, relief flooding through her veins.

"Yeah, sorry, Juniper," Seed says sheepishly. "You okay?"

Seed, Dandelion, Maple, and Dahlia appear over her with looks of concern on their faces.

"I'm fine. How about you? Dandelion, Seed? Are either of you hurt?"

The hedgehog shakes his head, smiling widely. "You're my hero."

FAILURE AND FORGIVENESS

"What he said," Dandelion grins.

The cadets continue marching through the forest for what feels like hours without finding the clearing Maple and Dahlia had spotted.

"I think we've gotten turned around somehow," Juniper admits, scratching an itchy spot between her ears. "Maple, how about we find a better vantage point and figure out where we are?"

The woodpecker agrees. Dahlia and Seed, already marked with the Archer's red stamp and thus out of the exercise, keep Dandelion company on the ground while Juniper and Maple attempt a reconnaissance mission. The squirrel scurries up the nearest tree while the woodpecker spreads his wings.

"There it is! About a mile that way!" Juniper shouts from her perch atop a small fir tree, pointing to a small clearing in the distance.

"I see it!" Maple whoops with excitement. Juniper freezes. Just over the last of the woodpecker's loud squawks, Juniper hears something that makes her blood run cold.

Keee-errr.

That terrible sound is permanently etched into the corners of her mind. *It can't be—can it? The hawk from The Waste... here?*

Keee-errr.

"Juniper, watch out!"

Maple attempts to dive into the branches

beneath them to dodge the hawk's awful, outstretched talons, but he doesn't make it in time. Juniper watches in horror as the large bird of prey gets a forceful hold of the woodpecker for one split second before releasing him, apparently realizing it has missed its target. Juniper screams when she sees her friend's limp body plummet to the forest floor below. She takes a blind flying leap to lower branches, just missing the hawk as it circles back for a second attack. Juniper hears its chilling shriek of disappointment overhead when she disappears into the darkness beneath the blackberry vines.

Dandelion, Seed, and Dahlia are already huddled around Maple when Juniper makes it back to the ground.

Maple groans. "I think my wing is broken."

"I think you're right." Juniper grimaces at the sight of white bone jutting through black feathers. She rummages through her knapsack and fashions a sling from a strip of tent canvas.

"Let's use the cot as a stretcher," Dahlia suggests.

"Great idea," Juniper agrees, thankful she was stubborn enough to bring her knapsack after all.

Dahlia and Dandelion help arrange Maple comfortably on the stretched canvas. The sun is setting when the four weary cadets lift the make-shift gurney to continue the journey. "I think we've just got one more mile to go, give or take." Juniper attempts to rally them for the last leg.

"Go ahead without me," Maple croaks sadly. "You will never get there in time."

"We're not going to leave you behind. Don't worry, we'll make it." Juniper promises, but she isn't so sure.

The last mile is the hardest. Just when Juniper doesn't think she can take another step, she spots dots of flickering candlelight in the distance.

"Come on! We're almost there!"

Sergeants Pine, Clover, and Pollen run out to meet them and take over Maple's care.

In the dark, Juniper can see outlines of six empty chairs where the hostages had been tied for the exercise. Her stomach sinks when she realizes they are too late.

Turning to find her friends, she bumps into a gray squirrel.

"Ash!"

At the sight of her foster brother, Juniper falls to her knees, overcome with a mixture of grief, relief, and exhaustion.

"Ash, I'm so sorry," she mumbles into her paws. "We failed you." Juniper's shoulders shake with sobs. "I failed you."

"Hey, come on. Don't be so hard on yourself," he

says, gently helping Juniper to her feet. "You did the right thing. I'm the one that failed—I'm the one that should be apologizing."

Juniper throws her arms around Ash.

"I am so sorry, Juniper. Will you please forgive me?"

"I think I forgave you a long time ago." Juniper says, surprised by the words that come out of her mouth. She is even more surprised to realize she actually means them. The day's events had shifted her perspective, leaving her confused mind sharper, clearer. Just last night, she'd asked herself if she would be able to trust Ash again, but deep down she'd really been wondering if she could trust herself. "All this time, I've been angry with myself—for not being there when the weasels came."

There is a long silence before Ash speaks. "Sometimes, it's easier to be angry with others than to carry the blame ourselves."

"Where'd you hear that?"

"Jasper." He shrugs sheepishly.

"Huh. He's smarter than he lets on."

Ash laughs.

One by one, the cadets are beckoned into a large tent where Colonel Thistle and the rest of their instructors, including Jasper, are waiting for them at a long table. Juniper is surprised to see Uncle Hemlock, the general, seated next to Colonel Thistle when she ducks through the tent flap. The cardinal calls Juniper to stand at attention before them. She is embarrassed to feel hot tears in the corners of her eyes. She doesn't want to disappoint her brother and uncle with the news of her failure.

"Even though you failed the mission..." Colonel Thistle begins. A rogue teardrop slides down Juniper's cheek. "You passed the exercise."

"Wait, what?" Juniper opens her mouth in disbelief.

"Your character will serve you—and the Archers—well, Cadet Spark. Congratulations. We'll see you at graduation in the morning."

"Thank you, sir," Juniper squeaks in a trembling voice. She gives her uncle an incredulous look, and he winks.

Juniper's knees feel like jelly when Oak, the pine marten, brushes past her on her way out of the tent. A few moments later, she hears what sounds like muffled arguing through the tent canvas.

"But I made it hours before the others. I completed the mission—" She hears Oak start to protest, but the colonel interrupts.

"At the expense of your fellow recruits. Even though you completed the mission successfully, you failed the exercise. You still have more training to do, Cadet Oak. You will not be graduating tomorrow."

A mixture of sadness and gratitude swirls inside Juniper's chest when she joins the others for a celebratory meal of pumpkin soup, roasted pine nuts, and dried apples around the campfire, fully aware of the mercy she has been given.

THIRTEEN
GRADUATION DAY

Spirits can't be dampened by the rain and mud that sully the march back to Camp Marshall the following morning. Weeks of rigorous training have come to an end, and in just a few short hours, the new recruits will pin on the rank of lieutenant and be welcomed into the exclusive Order of the Archers.

Juniper's hunch had been right. They *had* been walking in circles to draw out their initial hike to the campsite. Today's trek back to the barracks takes a third of the time, although the blisters on her paws make the distance feel much longer than it actually is. She cannot wait to get this day over with and be back at Logan Bramble, in her own tent, by nightfall.

When Camp Marshall comes into view, the troops head straight for the barracks. Pecan shell halves filled with rainwater are waiting at each bunk.

"Make yourselves presentable, cadets!" Sergeant Pollen announces before ducking out of the tent.

Before Juniper dips her paws in the cool water, she catches a glimpse of herself in the dim reflection.

For a moment, she doesn't recognize the young squirrel staring back at her. Lean muscles define her cheekbones, arms, and shoulders. In just one month of focused discipline and dedication, she has become visibly stronger. Also dirtier.

"I'm so excited!" Dahlia squeals as she splashes water on her face.

Juniper grins. "Same here. I can't wait to have a decent meal."

"Yes, no more lumpy pudding or mystery porridge!"

Juniper laughs, daydreaming about Sorrel's piping hot acorn casserole while she scrubs away the last of the mud caked to her fur.

The Archer band begins to play when the eleven graduating recruits march to the crowded parade field. Juniper had heard the Song of the Archers before, but she has never experienced an emotional response to its rhythm until this moment. She can feel the music swirling in her chest, set to the tempo of the claps and cheers of family members and friends filling the wooden stands on either side of the long stretch of green moss. It seems as if the whole Bramble has come to celebrate the newest Archers.

From the corner of her eye, Juniper spots Poppy, her two-year old foster sister, in the blur of faces before anyone else. She is bouncing up and

GRADUATION DAY

down in the wooden stands, squealing "Juni! Juni!"

"Wow! Is that your family?" Seed whispers. He is marching next to her, his tiny legs working harder than others' to stay in sync.

Juniper beams and straightens her posture. The butterflies that had filled her stomach a moment before seem to have fluttered away at the sight of Sorrel, her foster siblings, Willow, Rhodie, Sitka, Flint, and Hickory. Her family.

"Yes," she whispers back.

"You're so lucky!"

A pang of sadness fills Juniper's heart when she remembers many of the recruits will not have family members show up to celebrate their achievement today, or any other day. She tucks this realization away to remember later, wanting to soak up the bittersweet gift of this moment.

The ceremony is brief and poignant. Captain Spark brings the cadets to a halt and calls them to attention at the center of the parade field, where a small podium has been constructed. The music comes to a stop when Colonel Thistle steps onto the wooden platform and raises his wing. A hush falls over the excited crowd.

"Good afternoon. We are honored to have General Hemlock join us for today's graduation ceremony. Please give him a warm welcome."

A round of applause erupts when the large

squirrel joins Colonel Thistle on stage.

"Thank you all," he says in a gruff voice. "We are here today to recognize the commitment the cadets standing before us have made for the good of all of Mirren. The last four weeks have been a test of their strength and resilience. They have demonstrated their understanding of the Values and duties of the Archers."

General Hemlock turns to address the recruits directly, his eyes settling on the rows of disciplined climbers, fliers, burrowers, and rangers. "Today, you are no longer cadets. You have each earned the proud rank of lieutenant. Congratulations to you and your families."

Each new Archer is called to the platform to receive their triangular wooden badge. A loopy L is carved in the center, indicating their classification. Juniper cheers loudly for each of her friends, especially those like Daphne, Spike, and Seed who she knows do not have many guests present to celebrate them. A knot of emotion fills Juniper's chest when it's her turn to cross the stage.

"Well done," Sergeant Pollen says, pinning the rank of lieutenant onto her quiver. Colonel Thistle gives her a nod and a firm handshake, and she expects the same from her uncle. To her surprise, the general wraps her in a tight hug instead.

"I'm so proud of you, Juniper," he says, trying to

GRADUATION DAY

hide the emotion in his voice. "I wish your father could be here. He would be beaming."

Juniper smiles so widely her mouth begins to ache. As many times as she's heard similar sentiments in the last few weeks, she half-expected to be tired of it by now, but she's not. She now knows she could never grow tired of hearing how proud her father would be of who she is becoming.

When each new Archer has returned to their place on the parade field, Colonel Thistle draws the ceremony to a close. "Before you're dismissed, please report to Sergeant Pollen to receive your unit assignments. Your family and friends will be waiting for you in the stands. Excellent work, lieutenants."

At the nod of Colonel Thistle's beak, the recruits stomp in celebration. Juniper joins in whole-heartedly this time. When the thunder subsides, the Archer band ramps up again, and the sergeants wave the new lieutenants over to learn whom they will be serving alongside.

"Ash, you're with Captain Spark," Sergeant Pollen announces over the triumphant tunes and excited chatter. "Juniper, Dahlia, Spike, and Seed—you're rounding out Daphne's new team."

"Wait. You mean... I'm not with Jasper?"

"We can't afford to have you both in the same squad. It's too risky. What if you were attacked at the same time?"

Juniper blinks in surprise. She realizes, up to this moment, the cadets have just been playing war games. From now on, it wouldn't be blunt arrows and strawberry syrup. Cold disappointment fills her stomach, and another emotion adds on another layer of frost: fear.

Juniper doesn't have much time to dwell on her assignment. A pair of tiny arms wrap around her leg, giving her a tight squeeze.

"Juni!"

"Poppy! I'm so happy to see you!" She bends to pick up the toddler, who had proven herself to be her biggest, if not loudest, fan in the stands today.

Birch, Dougie, and Fern follow suit, with Sorrel, Rosie, and the rest trailing closely behind.

"Let's make a Juniper sandwich!" Birch shouts excitedly.

A crowd of smiling, familiar faces wraps around Juniper like a warm quilt, and she folds into their embraces. Feelings of relief, joy, and pride warm her from the inside out.

Juniper doesn't confront her brother until she has had the opportunity to hug and thank each of her family members and friends. "Did you know we wouldn't be together?"

Jasper folds his arms and raises an eyebrow, assuming a defensive position.

"Why didn't you say anything? You just let me

assume..." Juniper continues in an accusatory tone.

"I didn't let you do anything, little sister. I can't read your mind, and I have no control over what you presume." He says coolly, eager to change the subject. "Hey, I have a surprise for you. C'mon."

Juniper follows her brother to her tent in a huff. Her sour attitude dissolves as soon as her eyes adjust to the transition to softer light and a set of wooden armor comes into view. Its elegant silhouette appears slightly more delicate and detailed than Jasper's—and much smaller.

"I had it sized for you, so you won't be able to put this one on backward, even if you tried."

"What? I was expecting another prank!" Juniper shakes her head in disbelief. "It's beautiful! Is it really mine?"

Jasper nods.

"Jasper... I don't know what to say. Thank you so much." Juniper beams, reaching out her paw to touch the smooth, polished surface. "I can't wait to wear it."

"That's great," Jasper puts a heavy hand on her shoulder. "You're being briefed on our first mission in an hour. Time to suit up."

The celebratory meal Juniper had been daydreaming about would have to wait; however, as usual, Sorrel's intuition had not left her unprepared. "I expected you might be needed sooner than later," she says quietly, giving Juniper a reluctant hug after she'd already said her goodbyes to the other family members. "I've heard whispers."

Juniper catches a glimpse of concern in her foster mother's eyes when she draws back to retrieve something from her apron pocket. "Here, I brought you something, just in case. Lavender tea cakes with raspberry butter."

Warmth radiates through the cloth they are wrapped in when Sorrel places them in Juniper's paws. Her mouth begins to water instantly.

"I will be praying for you, June," Sorrel says, giving her one last squeeze.

Juniper reluctantly plants a kiss on her foster mother's cheek before turning to follow her fellow Archers. The comforting warmth of promised prayers lasts longer than the steam rising from the teacakes. She can't shake the feeling she's going to need them.

FOURTEEN

RICHIE GORGE

Juniper senses the tension as soon as she steps into the tent. Candles flicker, casting gold-rimmed shadows on the canvas walls. General Hemlock and Captain Thistle are a sight to behold, standing behind the general's great desk in full battle armor.

Juniper observes the unusual war map laid out before them: a sand table with wooden pieces positioned around Mirren's landmarks. She recognizes The Waste, Jacob's Lair, and the strange, mountainous area to the northeast she remembers from the classroom map: Richie Gorge.

Juniper squeezes between Dahlia and Daphne, joining her squad around the table. "Ouch!" Daphne grunts. Juniper realizes she's knocked the bobcat in the elbow. "Sorry," she whispers sheepishly. It will definitely take some time getting used to the clinking and clanking of the wooden armor plates trimming her frame—time she realizes she might not have.

Captain Thistle gets right down to business. "Lieutenants, your first assignment is a rescue mission. We're heading to Richie Gorge at dawn." The cardinal produces his stick from under the table and draws an invisible circle around the location in the air.

"We've received intel through Sergeant Sitka," he continues. "We've vetted it, done thorough reconnaissance, and it seems to be good information."

General Hemlock locks eyes with the bobcat standing next to Juniper. "Lieutenant Daphne, because your team is so green, you will be accompanied by two other units. Captain Spark and Sergeant Pine will each lead a group of soldiers, and Sergeants Pollen, Clover, and Moss will be guiding yours."

"There will also be a medical unit set up in an abandoned rabbit hole in a grove of dead trees that lies here." Colonel Thistle points to an unmarked area on the map where the desert Waste meets the rocky mountains at the base of Richie Gorge.

Juniper swallows hard when Hemlock begins to explain the plan. "There appears to be a prison of sorts inside the Gorge." He points to a sliver in the jagged face of the mountain. "We believe this is the only entrance."

"Is it guarded?" One of the new lieutenants asks, although Juniper can't see over the furry ears and feathery heads crowded around hers to find out who spoke. She guesses it was Daphne.

"Heavily," the general replies in a tone that suggests he's not annoyed by the seemingly silly question. "Weasels keep watch at the entrance of the gorge and patrol within the prison itself. Coyotes prowl the perimeter, and falcons and hawks cover the airspace."

"Word has it, one of the prisoners is Lieutenant Colonel Hawthorn Spark, who has been missing for fourteen years," Colonel Thistle says.

Juniper's heart jumps into her throat. She looks at her brother, who is standing next to their uncle on the other side of the sand table. He is staring at the map with a stoic look on his face. "The mission is to infiltrate the prison and bring him back to the Bramble."

"There is still a chance this is a trap, which is why it's such a risk to send two members of the Spark family," the colonel says, and Juniper sees Jasper's jaw tighten.

Feeling eyes on her, she looks around at the room full of Archers. Her knees begin to tremble when she realizes each one of them is risking their life for her father's. She is overwhelmed with gratitude.

"Daphne, your team is charged with holding the south side of the perimeter." The cardinal moves on. "You will take cover in the grove of dead trees and ready your bows from a distance."

"Sergeant Pine's troops will head around the

Gorge to secure the north side. Captain Spark's group will be heading straight into the ravine."

Juniper accepts a long, hooded cloak from Sergeant Clover as he issues one to each Archer. The icy blue cloth is thick but lighter than it looks.

"Winter has already reached the northeastern corner of the island," Hemlock answers the questions already forming in Juniper's mind. "Conditions will be harsh. We expect there to be significant amounts of snow and ice. The predators are used to hunting and fighting in these temperatures."

"These cloaks will help camouflage you in the mountains and also protect you from the bitter cold," the general explains. "We head out at first light."

Juniper shivers despite the air feeling warm and stuffy thanks to the number of Archers crowded into the general's tent. The briefing concludes with the clanging of wooden armor muffled by heavy cloth as the Archers work to put on their cloaks in the cramped space. When Juniper steps out into the night air, she takes a deep breath, relishing the feel of the cold, damp breeze tousling her fur.

"I believe these are yours, Lieutenant Spark," a voice from behind causes her to jump. She turns to find Colonel Thistle carrying the dagger and amber necklace.

Juniper sighs with relief as she accepts her possessions from his outstretched wing.

"Godspeed," Colonel Thistle replies. When Juniper looks up to thank him, she realizes he has already disappeared into the general's tent.

Juniper's whole body tenses. She can't help but remember her first trek across the Waste when Sergeants Pollen, Clover, and Moss lead her team into the dry riverbed at dawn the next morning. This is the way they'd come when she'd accompanied Jasper, Sitka, Rhodie, and Willow on a mission to find Flint the Black, the last-known surviving member of the First Alliance. He also happened to be a grizzly bear.

A shiver runs down her spine and up to the tip of her tail when she remembers having her first run in with the red-tailed hawk in this very spot. It had come for *her*, but it ended up with Rhodie instead. Thankfully, Willow had rescued the field mouse and brought her back safely to their hiding spot in a cave near Jacob's Lair.

This time, the troops make it to the other side of the Waste without incident. The grove of dead trees is easy to spot. Medics get to work constructing the field hospital in the abandoned rabbit hole while the three additional units begin to set up camp.

It is nearly dark when the teams are given permission to rest. Juniper hasn't had much time to talk to Rhodie, Willow, or Sitka since the graduation ceremony, and she finds them sitting together at the base of a rotting poplar. It feels strange to see Ash seated among them, devouring one of the lavender tea cakes Sorrel had given him as well. Willow is drinking her fill of nectar from a withering flower bud, and Rhodie is nibbling a dried strawberry when Juniper joins them on the hard ground.

"Hey, hey! If it isn't the prophesied red squirrel who's going to save us all!" Sitka yanks off a piece of the earthworm jerky he's eating and pops it into his smiling mouth. Juniper laughs, remembering the primal fear that overcame her the first time she'd laid eyes on the fox. So much has changed since then.

"Right," she says, rolling her eyes. "I'm going to take down the predator army by myself with this thing." Juniper pulls the dagger from its sheath on her hip. The amber stone picks up the flickers of the nearby campfire.

"I'm sorry about the unit assignments," Ash says with his mouth full, walking right over the eggshells others had been tiptoeing around all day. Juniper blushes.

"It's fine... really." She fumbles to unfold the cloth wrapped around her own teacakes. "I get why we have to be separated." She raises the small treat to her mouth and takes a bite. Another one of Sorrel's proverbs comes to mind. *It's easier to look on the bright side when there's food in your belly.* Juniper smiles.

"Honestly, I'm glad you're the one stuck with Jasper," she says with her cheeks full of crumbs. "Spending so much time with both of you would not be good for my sanity."

Her friends' laughter helps to further lighten the mood.

"Can't sleep either?" Another wave of deja vu washes over Juniper when she joins her brother by the campfire after the rest of the camp seems to have settled in for the night. He shakes his head, and she takes a seat next to him. The temperature is already dropping rapidly, and the warmth of the crackling flames feels good on the tips of her chilled ears and nose.

"I've been meaning to share something with you," she says, rubbing her paws together. Juniper retrieves her mother's most recent letter from her knapsack and passes it to her brother. It is already crumpled from the number of times she has read and reread the words.

Jasper's eyes drift across the page, his expression unchanging. When he is finished, he folds the paper and hands it back to her. "You know, it bothers me that she sent you letters. I never got any... why *you* and not me?"

The question stings. It feels as though Jasper thinks it's her fault somehow. She retorts without thinking. "It bothers me that you got to grow up knowing who you are, who your family is... you got to go to Bramble Academy and grow up with Hemlock."

"While we're being honest, I'm jealous you got to grow up with Sorrel. Hemlock isn't very motherly, if you hadn't noticed," Jasper smirks.

Heavy clouds of silence hang over their heads for a moment. Juniper realizes blood isn't the only thing they share. Jealousy runs in their veins too.

"This isn't a competition, you know," she says.

Jasper nods, staring into the fire. After a while, Juniper is brave enough to ask a question she's been holding on to for a while.

"Do you remember anything about our parents?"

Jasper is silent just long enough to make Juniper think he's ignoring her.

"I was barely three years old when they left, so I don't remember much," he finally speaks in a quiet voice. Jasper clears his throat before continuing. "I remember living in a place with sunshine, warmth, and lots of green grass... the sound of running water and birds twittering. Not the annoying kind—the chirping that sounds like music."

"I remember Dad's laugh and Mom's belly growing," he continues. "She let me put my paw on her fur so I could feel you move. It was the weirdest thing ever. Like a grub wiggling around in there."

Jasper laughs, but there is a hollow sound to its usual playfulness. Sadness shines in his eyes. "You looked like a little bald rat when you were born."

Juniper smiles and lets tears roll down her cheeks.

"And then... it all happened so fast. I remember the Unraveling in blurs of color, action, and noise... nothing specific really. My first real memories are being with Hemlock at Logan Bramble. Going to school. Training. Learning the ways of the Archers."

Although Juniper's experiences growing up without her parents aren't the same as Jasper's, she realizes for the first time that she can relate to him on a level that many would not be able to understand. Juniper puts her arm around her brother's shoulders and is surprised to find he lets her leave it there. She closes her eyes, feeling safe for the first time in recent memory, and falls asleep on his arm.

The Archers eat breakfast in silence before forming their units and preparing to take their assigned places around Richie Gorge.

"This is where we part ways," Jasper says when Juniper finds him in the crowd to wish him luck one last time. His team is the one tasked with infiltrating the prison to rescue their father, and she is numb with fear for all of them.

"Be safe," she says, trying to hide the trembling

in her voice. "Love you, brother."

"You too," he replies awkwardly.

Juniper hugs Rhodie, Willow, Sitka, and Ash before watching them disappear into the jagged rocks at the base of the Gorge. When she can no longer spot Jasper's orange tail, Juniper turns to find her place with her own unit. She stops cold in her tracks when she hears Sitka's distinct shout and Rhodie's unmistakable squeal.

Juniper clambers up the nearest crumbling tree trunk and spots Jasper and his team trapped in a circle of boulders a few hundred yards away. The scene around them chills her to the bone: wiry mottled fur, bared yellow teeth, and dozens of sharp claws rush toward her brother and friends like a crushing wave.

"Jasper!" Juniper screams for her brother, alerting the troops still on the ground beneath her.

"We're under attack! They must've been tipped off!" Jasper shouts at Juniper from his position. "Change of plans!"

"What do you mean?"

"You must go! Find our father!" Jasper says. "Hurry!"

His voice is lost in a sea of growls and snarls.

FIFTEEN
FOUND & LOST

Snow is falling, but Juniper can't feel the cold. She is too focused on making it up the steep mountainside without slipping on icy rocks. Everything around her appears to be painted varying shades of gray and white. Even her own fur seems to have lost its bright orange hue.

"This way!" Sergeant Pollen shouts over his shoulder. Juniper and Seed follow him onto a ledge where snowflakes are already collecting in a thick blanket beneath their paws. "Richie Gorge is right around this cliff face. We'll wait here until we get the signal."

A hasty plan had been put in place, and Juniper and Seed followed Sergeant Pollen to a designated area near the prison entrance. Meanwhile, Sergeant Moss, the swallow, had taken off with Dahlia to put eyes on the predators guarding the prison entrance. On the ground, Daphne and Spike accompanied Sergeant Clover, the hare, to ambush the weasels and draw them away from the mouth of the Gorge to give Juniper, Daphne, and Seed a window to safely penetrate the prison walls and carry out the rescue mission.

Juniper can't help but count the seconds that pass since she last saw Dahlia, Daphne, and Spike. It's either that or dwell on the fact she doesn't know what's happening to Jasper, Ash, and their friends at the bottom of the mountain—and she definitely can't do that. When her own intrusive thoughts cause her to lose her place, she begins again.

Five-hundred-seventy-two...

Five-hundred-seventy-three...

Five-hundred... I wonder what's taking them so long? They should have been back by now. Ah, what number was I on again? Ugh. One...two...three...

Finally, Juniper spots Sergeant Moss and Dahlia overhead, a pair of dark ink spots on the colorless sky. The small bird and bat appear to grow larger as Juniper watches them come in for a landing.

"We're clear," Sergeant Moss announces when his scaly feet hit the ground. He ruffles his feathers to rid himself of the ice that had formed on his wings mid-flight. "The weasels are occupied, and Daphne and Spike have taken their places at the prison entrance—the bobcat standing guard at the gate, itself, and the squirrel hidden in the rocks with his bow trained on the opening, just in case any unexpected visitors show up."

Sergeant Pollen nods in approval. "Excellent. Okay, Juniper, Seed. It's up to you. Dahlia will meet you at the gate. When you retrieve Hawthorn, bring him back to this landing. We'll be waiting for you."

Juniper is encouraged by Sergeant Pollen's use of *when* not *if*. It makes her feel like they have a fighting chance this time, but she chooses not to think about it. She is learning hope is a slippery thing to hold onto in predator territory.

Juniper raises her hood to avoid dripping icicles and sprays of frigid water coming at her from all directions. She presses her back to the rock wall and inches sideways, comforted little by the fact that each shuffle puts her one step closer to the cavernous prison entrance and further away from the narrow landing behind her where Daphne and Spike are standing guard at the wooden gate. There is nothing but a steep cliff between Juniper's paws and the rushing water below. It hisses at her like a contentious snake.

"Everything has gone to plan thus far. Just a few more steps!" Daphne calls encouragingly in their wake, sensing Juniper's apprehension.

Juniper can see Dahlia now. She is perched on a rock at the cavern entrance, the outline of her small black form barely visible against the obsidian rock behind her. It's sooty, shiny, and sharp—like burned ice.

"Come on!" The tiny bat beckons her friends, disappearing into the prison. Juniper takes a deep breath before ducking into total darkness, bracing herself for the chill and stench that waits inside. Seed follows her lead.

Between a brief moment of total blindness and the second Juniper's eyes adjust to the murky light, her senses are overwhelmed by putrid smells and the wild sound of her own heart beating loudly in her ears. When her eyes focus on the stone walls around her, she realizes there are no candles or torches to light the way. Darkness swallows them, broken only by thin strands of light that have made it through the narrow slit behind them. She is shocked at the number of stone bars that line the walls, marking rows upon rows of individual prison cells.

How many prisoners have been kept in the dark here—and for how long?

"Dahlia, I'm going to need you to be our eyes in here," Juniper says quietly. "Or is it ears? When this is all over, you're going to have to tell me how echolocation works."

In any other circumstance, Dahlia would have giggled. Recognizing her nocturnal abilities give her team an advantage in the pitch-black cave, she takes the lead. "Follow the sound of my voice!"

"Hawthorn? Hawthorn Spark?" Dahlia calls out

as they pass what look like shapeless lumps of fur behind the stone bars. "Hawthorn Spark? Do you know if he's here?"

Most of the imprisoned animals mumble or groan an incoherent response, but some manage to croak out something that sounds like, "No, sorry... please take me instead!" Over and over again, prisoners plead with frail, trembling voices, using what little strength they have to utter hopeful requests.

Juniper's spirits rise when a chipmunk with matted brown fur meets them at the bars of his prison cell in response to Dahlia's call. "Do you have anythin' to eat? I'll tell ya what I know if yer gimme summin' to eat."

Before Juniper has a chance to apologize for not having food to share, Seed removes a dried strawberry from beneath his small wooden helmet and passes it through the bars. The chipmunk accepts the treat with paws twisted by overgrown claws and begins to munch loudly.

"Can you tell us what you know about Hawthorn?" Seed asks gently.

The chipmunk's bulging cheeks look ridiculously large on his emaciated face. "Nope. Never heard of him," he says before disappearing into the shadows of his prison cell.

Juniper feels breathless and nauseous, like she's

been punched in the stomach. She remembers the moment she and Jasper discovered their mother was no longer hiding out in Jacob's Lair after their treacherous trek across The Waste to find her. Her heart sinks, realizing every step she takes down the long hallway leads further and further away from the dream of finding her father. *Would Jasper be able to withstand that kind of heartbreak again? Would I?*

"I'm sorry, Juniper..." Seed's voice is full of disappointment.

"Let's just keep going," she replies flatly.

The air grows colder and dryer, and Juniper wonders if the prison is leading them to the very heart of the mountain.

"Young lady... did you say Hawthorn?" A gruff voice calls from one of the prison cells on the right.

"Yes," Juniper says, stopping in her tracks. "Hawthorn Spark." She turns and takes one step towards the source of the voice.

"I haven't heard that name in a long, long time..." he begins to reply, but a coughing fit interrupts him.

"Do you know if he's here?" She presses her face to the stone bars and squints in the darkness, straining to see who she is speaking with.

"He's down at the end, love," his voice finally rasps, punctuating the sentence with a rattling hack. "The last cell."

Hope surges through her veins, and she

suddenly feels warm in spite of the numbing cold.

"Thank you, sir!"

Juniper and Seed race forward blindly. Dahlia's fluttering wings make an eerie slapping sound ahead of them in the dark. "This is it!" She announces. "The last cell."

Juniper knocks awkwardly on the stone bars, realizing she hadn't allowed herself to plan what she'd do in this moment if she ever made it this far.

"Excuse me," she begins, unsure of what to say next. She can hear her own voice, as if she is watching the scene unfold from a distance. "Do you know Laurel Spark? I'm her daughter," she says. "I'm looking for my father. His name is Hawthorn."

A pulsing silence swells in the darkness. Juniper's heart drops into her stomach. She holds her breath.

"Juniper... I've been praying every day that you would find me."

The squirrel, the hedgehog, and the bat respond with a long moment of stunned silence. Dahlia is the first one to shake off the shock and spring into action.

"We're going to get you out of here!" She squeaks.

"I'm on it!" Seed swiftly removes one of his spines and begins working the wooden lock. "Aw, nuts and berries! My quill snapped in half."

"Seed, hurry!" Juniper urges.

"Almost got it..." Juniper can hear Seed picking the lock with a second hedgehog spine. "Almost got it..."

There is a loud click and clatter when the lock falls onto the stone floor.

Juniper's stomach flips when the door gives way beneath her elbows. She reaches out into the darkness to help her father stand, and he collapses onto her instead. With little effort, she lifts him into her arms like an infant. He feels light and fragile, like dry twigs covered in dry moss, and his fur smells of earth and decay. She can hear a rattling sound like acorns bouncing around in his chest. He wheezes with every breath.

"Ponth. Borif. Comer." His words are muffled in the thick cloth of her cloak.

"What?"

"Pouch. Buried. Corner."

"Seed, I think he's trying to tell us there's something buried in the corner. Can you see what it is?" Seed roots around in the dark and finds a soft spot in the floor where a hole has been filled with crushed stone.

"Got it!" He says when he produces a small pouch from the rubble. Juniper takes it from him without inspecting it and slides it beneath her chestplate.

"Let's go!" Dahlia shouts.

A shaft of sunlight pierces the darkness. Juniper holds her father's body close to her chest as she passes the narrow ledge and makes it through the wooden gate. Her stomach twists when she realizes Daphne and Spike are nowhere to be seen.

"Juniper!" Seed shrieks.

Juniper looks up in horror to see a flash of talons. Instinctively, she covers her father's limp body with her cloak, throwing her arms over her head to protect herself from the attack. There is a forceful slash, and hot pain shoots through her back. She reaches for her slingshot instead of her bow, and it clatters to the ground. Her fingers are numb from the cold. Force knocks her back, and she is suddenly clinging to the rocky cliff ledge, leaving her father exposed and vulnerable on the ground a few feet away from her. The sound of the water is too loud, too close. She looks down and her heart pounds fiercely.

"Juniper! I've got him!" Dahlia screeches, hurtling through the air. She lands at Hawthorn's side, covering him with her soft, black wings.

A larger pair of wings beat toward her with such force and wind, Juniper believes this must be the end. She squeezes her eyes shut and braces herself for the impact she knows is coming. There is a strong tug at her hip and then... nothing.

Juniper opens her eyes just in time to see a glint

of amber slip from its place on her belt. She looks on in horror as it clatters down the side of the cliff, disappearing into the foaming whitewater below. The hawk nosedives after it.

A wave of nausea overcomes Juniper when she realizes the redhawk isn't after her or her father—it wants the dagger. She reaches for an exposed root when a flash of red fur appears above her.

"Juniper! You're alive!"

Sitka gently closes his teeth around the nape of her neck and tosses her into the air. Juniper lands on all fours, her limbs trembling on solid ground.

Sitka reads the panic written all over her face. "What's wrong?"

Juniper blinks in disbelief. Her paw reaches for the belt where the dagger should be. Grief grips her chest.

"The dagger... it's gone."

SIXTEEN
SITKA'S SECRET

Before Juniper has time to explain, Sitka's sleek form seems to have multiplied. Juniper wonders if she hit her head in the fall. *Am I seeing double?* There are two foxes now—only, the second looks like a nightmarish version of her kind yet sarcastic friend.

"What are you doing, big brother?" Scary Sitka growls, and Juniper notices the scar. The scene in the woods with Flint flashes through her mind. When the fox attacked them on the way back from visiting Foster Hollow, the grizzly bear had driven it away with a single slash to its left ear.

"Get out of here, Spruce," Sitka snarls. "This isn't going to end well."

"Sitka, what's going on?" Juniper shouts confusion.

"Willow!" Sitka calls, his eyes wide. Even from a distance, Juniper can see the desperation in them.

To her surprise, the hummingbird seems to materialize at the sound of Sitka's voice. Her tiny wings are invisible as she hovers over the Gorge.

"The predator army is on its way to Logan Bramble right now! You have to tell Flint!"

"What? But, how?" Willow begins to buzz, but Sitka cuts her off.

"Willow, hurry! Please!"

The hummingbird turns and disappears over the Gorge in a brilliant flash of red and green.

"Traitor!" Spruce seethes and lunges at Sitka's throat.

"Flint! Flint! Wake up!" A rainbow zig zags through the air. Willow pokes at Flint's fuzzy rear end.

"Oh, buzz off!" Flint swipes a heavy paw clumsily in her direction, as if aiming to swat a bothersome fly.

Zipping out of the way, Willow dashes back to Flint's cavernous ear. "No, Flint! WAKE! UP!" She pokes him again, this time on the bridge of his nose.

"I need you to stop doing that!" Flint growls.

"The predators... their army... they're on their way to the Bramble! Right now!"

Flint jumps onto all fours as if Willow had dumped ice cold water on him. Shaking the dreams from his head, Flint catches a terrible scent in the musty air of his dark lair.

He smells them before he hears them. He hears them before he sees them. The ground begins to shake with the pound of claws overhead. In a choking cloud of smoke and flames, the predator army descends upon Logan Bramble.

Juniper wakes on a cot in a dimly lit space. There is a damp, earthy smell to the air, and roots run down the walls around her like veins. At first, she doesn't remember the desperate trek down the mountain with her father's and Sitka's limp bodies. She can't recall the moment the medics had met her, Dahlia, and Seed at the mouth of the abandoned rabbit hole and taken the wounded away on stretchers.

When she sits up, she reaches for the dagger and grabs the empty sheath. Her heart drops into her stomach, and the awful scenes come flooding back to her.

"You found him," a familiar voice says from across the room.

Juniper turns to see Jasper sitting on a gurney, staring dazedly into the air in front of him while a young rabbit bandages his left arm. Red darkens the strips of cloth she is wrapping around his wound, and Juniper realizes it's not strawberry syrup this time.

Juniper nods, relief and worry swirling through her chest at the sight of her injured brother. "Yes. Can you believe it? Our father is alive."

Jasper's bottom lip begins to tremble, and he quickly changes the subject. "Ash is in surgery right now. He's in pretty bad shape. If he pulls through,

I don't think he'll ever walk again."

Juniper closes her eyes, and fear washes over her, followed by a rush of anger and sadness. She has never seen her brother in this state before, and she can't process his news about Ash. Not right now. *Surely, it can't be true.*

Thankfully, Rhodie appears in the doorway, bringing good news.

"Sitka's awake. We can see him now."

Jasper barely waits for the rabbit nurse to snip the cloth from the bandage roll before he stands up and heads off to find Sitka's room in the underground field hospital. Juniper and Rhodie follow closely behind him.

They walk quickly through a series of tunnels that seem to lead off in several directions. It doesn't take long for Juniper to feel lost in the rabbit burrow, but Jasper seems to know where he's going. Finally, he stops in front of a doorway where a sheet of canvas has been hung for the patient's privacy. Sitka's name and rank are scrawled on a plate of wood hanging on the doorframe.

When Juniper steps through the curtain, she is startled by the sight of her wounded friend. He looks small and weak lying on the cot in the middle of the dim room. Jagged stitches wrap around his throat like thorny vines, and the deep gash beneath them looks angry and swollen.

Juniper is happy to see Sitka's eyes open and alert. He attempts a weak smile when his friends gather around his gurney.

"I shouldn't be here," Sitka says in a hoarse voice. "I don't deserve it."

Rhodie climbs onto the scratchy blanket draped over the fox's knees. "Don't say that, Sitka," she squeaks. "I don't know what we'd do without your daily dose of snark and sarcasm." Rhodie tries to make Sitka smile, but he cringes with pain instead.

"What was all of that about back there, Sitka? What happened?" Juniper asks, placing her paw gently on his.

When Sitka's eyes meet Juniper's, the depth of despair she sees in them scares her.

"Juniper, I have to tell you something..." Sitka pauses as if wavering on his decision to speak the truth. "My father, Sedge... he's loyal to King Cypress. Spruce—the fox that did this to me—is my brother."

Juniper nods. "I know all of that already."

"You don't understand. Since we were pups, Spruce and I... we were trained to hunt you."

Juniper draws back her paw as if she'd accidentally touched a piece of glowing charcoal. The air is sucked from her lungs by an invisible force.

"What do you mean? You were trained to hunt me... how? Why?" She shakes her head in disbelief.

"I was sent to Logan Bramble as a spy. My

mission was to gather intel. Up until today... I've been leaking information..." Sitka winces. Juniper wonders if the pain is physical or emotional.

"That's how the predators knew we'd left the Bramble..." Jasper speaks for the first time in a hushed tone.

"Yes, and on our mission to find Flint... the coyotes and the hawk—they knew where we were, because..." Sitka appears to gag on the words in his mouth. "Because... I tipped them off."

Juniper looks at her brother and sees the storm brewing behind his eyes. "All this time... you were gathering intel," he says slowly, beginning to put the pieces together.

Sitka nods, pained.

Jasper closes his eyes for a moment. When he opens them, he turns and moves to exit the room without another word. Juniper feels like she's going to be sick. She glances at Rhodie, who is now trembling on the corner of the cot.

"Sitka," the field mouse's voice cracks, her eyes full of sorrow. "We trusted you. How could you do this?"

"I've made my choice," he begins to explain. "I saw the way you lived... your Values... and I turned..."

A hot tear streams down Juniper's cheek. Out of the corner of her eye, she sees a burst of color and commotion over her shoulder. She turns to see

Willow hovering over Jasper in the doorway. Her colorful feathers are tinged with black soot.

"The Bramble!" She says, her voice panicked and shrill. "It's burning!"

SEVENTEEN
JASPER'S JEALOUSY

Juniper struggles to keep up with Willow, Rhodie, and Jasper in a race through the dark, winding tunnels that all look the same. Her arms and legs burn with exhaustion, and she is afraid her muscles are going to give out beneath her.

A searing pain shoots through her head when they burst through the dark entrance of the rabbit burrow and into rays of sunlight. A crowd has already gathered on the edge of the grove, and the hummingbird, field mouse, and squirrels push through fur and feathers to find General Hemlock. A scream catches in Juniper's throat when she finally finds an opening and manages to catch a glimpse of what everyone else is straining to see. Black plumes of smoke are rising over the Dark Forest beyond The Waste.

It's true. Logan Bramble is on fire.

"We have to leave now! We have to save them!" Jasper shouts.

"No," Hemlock says firmly with sorrow in his

eyes. "Too many of us are wounded. Flint and the rest are prepared for this. We need to trust them. As soon as we're able, we'll move camp to Jacob's Lair."

Jasper opens his mouth to argue with the general, but he thinks better of it. Instead, he turns and disappears into the throng of soldiers behind him. Juniper follows.

"Jasper?" Juniper ducks beneath the tent flap she'd just seen her brother pass through. "Are you okay?"

She is startled when an arrow whizzes past her, barely missing her right ear. "You almost hit me!"

"If I'd wanted to hit you, I would've." Jasper removes another arrow from his quiver and aims at the canvas just over Juniper's head.

"Jasper, I'm so sorry about Sitka. The dagger. All of it. Please stop—"

Juniper feels the arrow's wake ruffle her fur when he takes his next shot.

"Sitka's been my best friend for as long as I can remember. I met him as a kit," Jasper says, his voice shuddering with anger and disgust. "How could he do this?"

Juniper doesn't know what to say.

"I feel so stupid," her brother continues. "He was right under my nose all this time, and I never suspected... his sole purpose for living was to get you caught in the predator's crosshairs."

Juniper lets that realization sink in for a moment. It's painful, yes, but there's something about Sitka's confession that doesn't sit well with her. *How can this be true?*

"He risked his life for me. For all of us," she replies sadly. "It appears he's made his choice."

General Hemlock enters the tent unannounced. A third arrow takes flight, and there's another narrow miss.

"Jasper, get yourself together, son," his uncle warns.

"What's going to happen to Sitka?" Jasper asks, lowering his bow.

"There will be a trial," Hemlock says. "He will go before the New Alliance, and they will decide what should be done with him. I'm truly sorry, Jasper. I need you to think clearly now. We have much to do, but first—I will take you to see your father."

"How is he?" Juniper asks, a surge of optimism swelling in her chest.

Hemlock swallows. "He's weak. He's been in bad shape for a long time. We can't get him to eat or drink." The general pauses to choose his words carefully. "I think he's held on just long enough to meet you."

Jasper is quiet for a moment, and then a dam appears to break inside of him. He snaps an arrow in half over his knee and launches his bow, quiver and all, across the tent.

"I feel like everything I've done up to this point... my whole life... was all about finding our father. What if..." Jasper huffs. He lowers his voice as if it might make it less likely. "What if he doesn't make it? I don't know what to do now."

Juniper reaches for her brother's arm, but he jerks it away.

"It should have been *me*," he says through clenched teeth. "*I* should've been the one that found our father. *I* should've been the one our great—grandfather left the dagger to—*the prophesied squirrel.*" Jasper says the last few words with mock admiration. "If *I'd* had the dagger, it would have never been taken."

Juniper reels from Jasper's verbal blow. Waves of shock and shame ripple through her body.

"Don't follow me," he barks. Juniper watches her brother storm out of the tent.

"He's right," she says, her throat closing around her words. "About everything."

"No. He doesn't mean that, kid." Hemlock puts a heavy paw on her aching shoulder, but the room continues to spin around her. "Jasper's angry. He just needs time."

What if we don't have enough time left?

Juniper opens her mouth to speak, but the

words die on her tongue.

EIGHTEEN

JUNIPER'S UNRAVELING

Juniper gently squeezes her father's hand. He doesn't look anything like the fierce warrior she'd pictured in her head. His orange fur is dull and mottled with gray, and his closed eyes are sunken into his skeletal face. Juniper strains to see his chest rise up and down with each shallow breath.

This isn't how it's supposed to be! She screams in her head. *It's not fair!*

Juniper had dreamt of the moment she would embrace her father for the first time since she was a little squirrel. He would sweep her up into his strong arms and twirl her around, laughing and beaming with joy. Instead, *she* had been the one to pick *him* up. There'd been running instead of twirling and fearful screams instead of joyful laughter.

The day's terrible scenes flash through Juniper's mind. She closes her eyes and covers her face with her paws, as if that might make the awful images disappear. Desperation slices at her heart like a knife, threatening to slash her strength and resolve apart, thread by thread.

What do I do now?

Memories of Sorrel's whispered prayers over her own bedside flicker in her mind like candlelight, and Juniper suddenly remember's Colonel Thistle's mysterious declaration in the classroom: *It is said the Maker of Mirren, our own Creator, dwells within the elements and beyond.*

Juniper sighs. *Can the Maker hear me now?*

It isn't so much the invisibility that causes doubt. There are plenty of things she can't see that exist—the air she breathes, the balance that helps her bound from limb to limb without falling, and the energy that causes plants to grow and seasons to change, just to name a few. In this moment, Juniper feels unseen, unheard, unimportant. Alone. Her own conflicting emotions are what make it difficult for her to believe.

"Here goes nothing," she says aloud and bows her head.

Creator, thank you for my father. Please watch over him, help him grow stronger, and let him know how much he is loved...

Juniper's eyes fly open when she remembers the pouch Seed had uncovered in her father's prison cell earlier that day. She'd tucked it beneath her chestplate and forgotten all about it. Slipping her paw beneath the polished wood, she removes it from its place against her heart and holds it up to the nearest candle. There is nothing special about the small, brown pouch. The cloth is stiff with caked mud and deteriorating from years of being buried in the damp, cold earth. She gently tugs at the drawstrings, and the strands disintegrate in her paws.

Juniper cautiously turns the pouch upside-down. Her breath catches in her throat when a piece of polished amber tumbles into her paw. It dangles from a string just like the matching necklaces she and Jasper wear. Juniper carefully lifts her father's head and slips the family stone over his ears, positioning the rock so it rests squarely on his heart.

"Please hold on, Dad," she whispers. "I'm going to make things right." Juniper plants a kiss on her father's forehead and stands to leave. His skin is cool beneath his thin fur.

Juniper follows the tunnels up to the campsite alone and collects her belongings from a nearby tent. She slips into her icy blue cloak and pulls up the hood, protecting herself from the frigid wind beginning to blow down from the jagged mountains above them. She puts on her pack and grabs her copy of the Book of Mirren, the one Sorrel had given her, before stepping out of the shelter.

Somewhere in the underground field hospital beneath her feet, Sitka is awaiting trial. Ash is recovering from surgery. Her brother is falling apart, and her father is barely hanging on.

Then there's the dagger.

It's all too much for Juniper to bear.

The young squirrel steps to the edge of the grove and watches soot rain down like snow over the Waste and what's left of the Dark Forest. The smell of charred wood burns her lungs.

Juniper hugs the Book of Mirren close. The weight of it feels comforting on her chest. The flicker of hope that had begun to burn wildly in her heart has gone out. Everything around her is hazy and confusing, and she realizes the Book is the only place where true hope can be found now.

The Light will once again overtake the darkness; until then, we must trust in faith to guide us, relying not on what we can see... The words repeat in her head.

Standing in cold mountain shadows, Juniper finds it difficult to remember the warmth of sunshine, but she trusts it's still there somewhere behind the clouds of smoke—just like she knows Richie Gorge lies beyond the steep cliffs towering above her. And somewhere in the rocky chasm, her grandfather is hiding.

Juniper takes one look back at the campsite and makes a silent vow not to return until she recovers what she lost.

EPILOGUE

The red hawk brushes flakes of snow from her wings. Ice crystals melt quickly on the stone floor beneath her talons. Lord Alder has his back to her, kindling the fire to a roar in the cavernous hearth on the far wall. His bushy orange tail twitches with agitation.

The badger, Lord Agate, is slumped in a chair with his eyes closed, drooling over a half-eaten meal. He jolts awake with a snort when the hawk drops the dagger onto the table.

"At last!" Lord Alder gives a triumphant shout when he turns to see the red hawk's gift. He snatches the dagger and holds it up, a triumphant, crooked grin stretching across his withered face. The amber stone catches the light of flickering flames, casting a yellow glow on the dingy cave walls around them.

"I don't know what the fuss is about," Agate yawns. "It's not much to look at, really."

"Hush, Aggie," Alder barks. "You've done well, Larkspur."

The red hawk bows before the squirrel. "There's more, Lord Alder," she says, keeping her eyes on the floor. "It's Hawthorn. They have him. Your son is alive, but barely."

With a pained howl, Hawthorn drives the dagger into the table, and a long, jagged crack forms in the wooden surface.

"Come now, Alder. It's been fourteen years. It's not likely he was ever going to see the light anyway," the badger scolds with a dry laugh.

There is a long silence before Lord Alder speaks again.

"No, I suppose you're right, Aggie." He sighs. "And the fox?"

"He'll live, I think," the hawk reports.

Lord Alder clicks his tongue with disapproval. "Sedge won't be happy about that. King Cypress will come after *his* throat next as payment for his son's betrayal."

The badger grunts in agreement.

"Thank you, Larkspur," Alder says, waving his paw dismissively. "That will be all."

The hawk turns and takes flight, disappearing into a white curtain of snow.

"Put on your cloak, Aggie. We shall share the news with King Cypress and his fleabags—we *finally* have the dagger. "

"Yes," Lord Agate flashes a greedy smile, his

EPILOGUE

sharp yellow teeth flickering in the firelight. "The trap is set. Let's just hope the girl takes the bait."

Here's a sneak peek of...

BOOK THREE
JUNIPER SPARK
AND THE RIVER LASTING

PROLOGUE

King Cypress' wicked howls of laughter echo off the stone courtyard walls. Nestled among Mirren's highest peaks, the balcony before the wolf's lavish den has a birds-eye view of the thick smoke enveloping the Dark Forest beyond the Waste. Flakes of snow and ash swirl together, performing a terrible, unnatural dance in the night sky. Lord Alder shivers when he steps out of the cold shadows and into the glow of a raging fire.

The king spots the red squirrel entering his grand hall, and his gold eyes sparkle with victory. "Alder, my friend. Have you heard? Logan Bramble has fallen!" His voice is amplified by arching stone walls.

Alder and Agate approach the wolf with reverence, flanked by his pair of crooked coyote commanders, Fleabane and Skullcap.

"Yes, my king," Lord Alder bows low, and his badger companion follows suit. "Excellent news."

"I expect my day is about to get even better. I understand you have something for me."

"I do." Without looking up, the squirrel produces

the wooden dagger from his cloak pocket, presenting it to the king with outstretched paws.

"Outstanding," King Cypress grins, revealing two rows of sharp teeth that match the amber stone's yellowish hue. "And the girl?"

"She will come for it, your highness."

The coyotes scoff in their places beside Alder and Agate and speak over one another.

"Why didn't you snatch her when you had the chance?" Skullcap snarls while Fleabane whines.

"She's supposed to be the one mentioned in the old owl's prophecy, right? Don't we need her to do her part with the Tree?"

"She needs to be *willing*—" Alder begins to explain, but Skullcap cuts him off.

"How do you know she'll come?"

The squirrel does his best to mask irritation with confidence in his trembling voice. "She's a Spark. If she's anything like her father—" Alder pauses mid-sentence to speak his next thought internally: *Or her grandfather, for that matter.* "She will do anything to get back what's been taken from her."

King Cypress stretches lazily on his rocky throne. "I'm tired of your excuses and delays, Alder. No more games. We drain the lake at winter's end, with or without the girl."

Agate and Alder exchange concerned glances.

"Yes, your highness. It will be done."

PROLOGUE

The screech owl braces herself against the icy winds blowing wildly across Dogwood Bay. She leans heavily on her wooden staff, her stiff joints aching with every hobbled step.

A twisting tower of smoke rises above the choppy waters. Although she can't see Mirren from her perch atop the rocky crags of its sister island, Azalea, she knows Logan Bramble is burning. She can smell the charred pine and scorched earth.

"Oleander, what are you doing out here?" A hooded red squirrel appears at the owl's side. "It's freezing! You're going to catch a—" Before she can finish her sentence, the squirrel's delicate paws fly to her mouth when she realizes what has driven the frail bird from her cozy roost. She cries out in shock when she spots the ominous black cloud swelling over the waves. "No. No, no, no..."

Oleander closes her eyes and clenches her beak before speaking the words she has been dreading for fourteen years: "The fight begins."

ACKNOWLEDGEMENTS

With deepest gratitude to...

My husband, Dan, for continuing to remind me why I write, and for cheering me on when I am tempted to give up my pen. My sons, Jacob, Logan, and Marshall, for teaching me more about the wonders of the world and the eternal significance of home and family. Meforya, for your endless patience, expertise, and attention to detail. My Dark Sky ladies, Nichole, Anna, Seneca, Cassy, and Syreeta; spending time in the wilderness with you has been life-changing and integral to Juniper's story. Gary and Angela, for raising me in faith and for the gift of a book-filled childhood. Ron, for being one of my loudest cheerleaders. Natalie B., for your love and selflessness. Debby, for your heart of gold. Kelly and Kim, for loving me as a daughter. Susan and Bob, for blessing me with your son and caring for me like your own. Rita, Terry, and Vicki, for your hearts for family and hospitality. Katherine and Deo, for a lifetime of prayers. James and Liz, for your gift of family history and heritage. Wynn, for your support and encouragement, and Sasha, for lending your beautiful voice to Juniper and her friends. The Cochran Family, Mary Ellen Sims, and Claudia Kirkwood for celebrating my books and sharing them with others. Members of my launch team, for your generosity; Book Two is here thanks to you. I love you all.

ABOUT THE AUTHOR

Courtney Woodruff is a communications professional living in Fort Worth, Texas with her husband and three sons. She was adopted as an infant and raised in the Piney Woods of east Texas. She set off an unexpected, decade-long adventure when her husband joined the Army, living in Germany and Washington State.

Courtney writes for children, caregivers, and families in the margins of her days. She loves to spend time with her family (especially outdoors or around a table), read biographies, travel, and stargaze with friends. Courtney received a master's degree in counseling with a focus on resilience. She has a heart for foster care, adoption, and military families, and she believes God does good, unimaginable things through our skills, stories, and passions—our fishes and loaves—when we give them away.

CONNECT WITH HER ON INSTAGRAM
@COURTNEYLWOODRUFF

ABOUT THE ILLUSTRATOR

Mehnaaz Husain is an Indian-based illustrator who is fiercely emotionally driven when it comes to storytelling. She was born in 2001 and brought up in Udaipur, the City of Lakes, in the desert state of Rajasthan. She loves creating art and the majority of her inspiration comes from her own experiences and the environment around her. She is very observant which translates well into the meticulous details in her works. From a very young age, she loved creating art in mediums that span digital, oil, acrylic and watercolors, for which she credits her grandpa, Yaqub, entirely. He always encouraged her and motivated her on her journey in her early years by taking her on countless scooter rides to art stationeries. She has been felicitated by numerous awards at local and national level for her craftsmanship in colors and words. She loves to illustrate for children by bringing text to life by giving it a visual form. Her other interests include animation, writing poetry and swimming. She is currently completing her bachelor's degree in Communication Design at National Institute of Design, AP, India and works as a freelancer in the field of publishing, illustration and animation

FIND HER ONLINE @MEFORYA & WWW.MEFORYA.COM

THE ADVENTURE CONTINUES...

Did you enjoy *Juniper Spark and the Unraveling*?

Please consider leaving an honest review on Amazon or Goodreads. Sharing positive feedback online is a great way to support authors and illustrators. Thank you so much!

Look for Book Three...

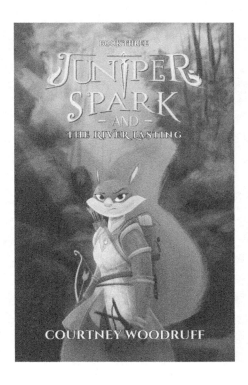

READ MORE FROM THE AUTHOR AT
WWW.AMAZON.COM/AUTHOR/COURTNEYWOODRUFF

Made in the USA
Monee, IL
02 October 2023

43840327R00111